P9-CQF-887

"Emily, get down from there!"

She turned her head and saw Tyler striding through the open door to her room. She returned her gaze to the window. "I can't see him. I don't know how he could have gotten away so fast."

"Now!" he said, clamping his hands on her hips. He lifted her off the window seat and swung her to the floor.

"You've got no reason to yell at me! I stayed put this time," Emily said.

"You were making yourself a target."

"I was trying to get a picture of him."

"Your story's not worth your life," Tyler said.

"It wasn't for my story. Having a photo of *el Gato* would help your mission."

"Dammit, Emily. You've got to be more careful."

The worry on his face was unmistakable. She understood how he felt—they'd been through this before. She put her palm on his cheek. "Tyler…"

He steadied her face between his hands and kissed her.

It knocked her breathless.

Dear Reader,

Ever since I wrote EYE OF THE BEHOLDER for my first *Eagle Squadron* series, I've been eager to return to the island paradise of Rocama that I created for the book. The tiny country has prospered during the years since Eagle Squadron destroyed the drug cartel that had corrupted the government. Tourism has become a major industry. Thus, when I began plotting ACCIDENTAL COMMANDO, Rocama seemed like the perfect spot to send my heroine on her honeymoon, especially since she was going without a groom. What better place for a jilted bride to heal her heart?

Of course, Emily Wright fought me every step of the way. She didn't believe her heart needed to heal. She was through with men, finished with love. All she wanted was peace and quiet. She definitely didn't want to get mixed up with a team of Delta Force commandos who needed her help to stop an assassin. So she fought Sergeant Tyler Matheson every step of the way, too.

Like Emily, Tyler wasn't looking for romance, he only wanted to complete his mission. He certainly didn't want to choose between his duty and a stubborn, troublesome woman....

I love giving characters what they *think* they don't want!

Happy reading,

Ingrid

INGRID
WEAVER

Accidental Commando

ROMANTIC
SUSPENSE

If you purchased this book without a cover you should be aware that this book is stolen property. It was reported as "unsold and destroyed" to the publisher, and neither the author nor the publisher has received any payment for this "stripped book."

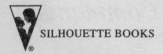

SILHOUETTE BOOKS

Recycling programs
for this product may
not exist in your area.

ISBN-13: 978-0-373-27684-4

ACCIDENTAL COMMANDO

Copyright © 2010 by Ingrid Caris

All rights reserved. Except for use in any review, the reproduction or utilization of this work in whole or in part in any form by any electronic, mechanical or other means, now known or hereafter invented, including xerography, photocopying and recording, or in any information storage or retrieval system, is forbidden without the written permission of the editorial office, Silhouette Books, 233 Broadway, New York, NY 10279 U.S.A.

This is a work of fiction. Names, characters, places and incidents are either the product of the author's imagination or are used fictitiously, and any resemblance to actual persons, living or dead, business establishments, events or locales is entirely coincidental.

This edition published by arrangement with Harlequin Books S.A.

For questions and comments about the quality of this book please contact us at Customer_eCare@Harlequin.ca.

® and TM are trademarks of Harlequin Books S.A., used under license. Trademarks indicated with ® are registered in the United States Patent and Trademark Office, the Canadian Trade Marks Office and in other countries.

Visit Silhouette Books at www.eHarlequin.com

Printed in U.S.A.

Books by Ingrid Weaver

INGRID WEAVER

Ingrid Weaver propped an old manual typewriter on her children's playroom table to write her first novel. Twenty-six books later there's a computer in place of the typewriter and a RITA® Award on the corner of her grown-up-sized desk, but the joy she found in creating her first story hasn't changed. "I write because life is full of possibilities," Ingrid says, "and the best ones are those that we make." Ingrid lives on a farm in southern Ontario, where she gardens in the summer and knits in the winter. You can visit Ingrid's Web site at www.ingridweaver.com.

To Mark,
who still makes life an adventure.

Chapter 1

Sergeant First Class Tyler Matheson lifted the scope away from his eye, ran his thumb around the rubber eyepiece collar to dry off the sweat, then flattened himself against the courthouse roof to sight on the plaza below. The sun wasn't yet up and already the day was promising to be a steam bath. The locals had started setting up their market stalls before first light, and now the cobblestones were getting clogged with everything from wheelbarrows of bananas to crates of live chickens. Stray dogs nosed among the carts while seagulls, drawn from the harbor by the promise of scraps, fluttered and swooped over the crowd. Picking out a lone assassin in that melee would be a challenge.

Jack Norton's voice came through Tyler's headset. Jack was positioned near the gates of the governor's palace on the far side of the plaza. "Someone's on the scaffold. You see him, junior?"

Tyler moved his rifle toward his left. A column of

steel pipes and wooden planks rose above the corner of the courthouse where the facade was being repaired. An ambitious restoration project was underway throughout Rocama City's historic Old Quarter, which included the colonial-era structures around this plaza in the heart of the district. It was meant to benefit the island nation's budding tourist industry. It didn't do much good for security. It was tough to lock down a site when there were so many uncontrolled vantage points.

Yet Eagle Squadron had been ordered to keep this mission low-key. There would be no change of routine, no road closures, no security zones or aerial surveillance. The Rocaman president's keenly loyal palace guards were their only backup. The real purpose of the American envoy's visit had to remain a secret until the official announcement could be made.

Tyler used his elbows to drag himself closer to the edge of the roof and centered the scope's crosshairs on the figure who was climbing the scaffold. The man wore a hard hat and a tool belt, so he could be a workman wanting to get an early start on the day. Tyler's hunter's instincts told him otherwise. The man's body language didn't jive with that of a guy getting paid by the hour. And he was moving too carefully, as if he were carrying more than what was visible. "That's our shooter," he said into his transmitter.

"Maybe." It was Duncan Colbert's voice. Judging by the volume of the squawking in the background, he was near the chicken crates. "The scaffold provides good line of sight for the entrance to the palace, but it leaves the shooter exposed."

"Doesn't matter. No one's looking up," Jack said. "There's too much action down here."

"He could be heading for your roof, junior," Duncan said. "It's the only flat one around."

"Or he could be checking out the brickwork before the rest of his crew comes in— Damn!" Jack said. "Did you see that jump?"

Tyler lifted his head. The man had disappeared from his scope. That was because he had leaped to the low roof of the adjacent building, the Royal Rocaman Hotel.

Tyler pushed to his feet, looped the strap of his rifle across his chest and sprinted to the far edge of the courthouse roof. He bypassed the scaffold and jumped, relying on his momentum to carry him directly to the hotel. He hit the tiles hard and grabbed the ridge along the peak to regain his balance just as his quarry slid down the slope of the roof and over the edge. Tyler listened for an impact or alarm from the ground, but there was none. He inched forward. "Where'd he go?"

"He landed on a balcony," Jack said. "Top floor of the hotel. Huh, just like a cat."

"The palm trees are blocking my view," Duncan said. "I'm going to change position."

"He's about three yards ahead of you, junior," Jack said. "I can't see his face."

Tyler moved forward three yards, then turned and slid headfirst down the tiles on his stomach until he caught the edge of the roof in his hands. He looked over.

A stocky man was beside a cluster of wrought iron furniture less than twelve feet below him. He'd discarded the hard hat and the tool belt and was kneeling on the floor, his dark head bent over his lap as he assembled a sniper's rifle.

Adrenaline punched Tyler's gut, just as it always did when he closed in on his quarry at the end of a hunt. Though no photographs of him existed, this had to be El Gato, the assassin Eagle Squadron had been ordered to stop. Intelligence hadn't expected him to strike so soon, since

the American envoy he was targeting would be in Rocama
City for more than a week if the talks went as scheduled, but
the team had wanted to cover all its bases. Could it really be
this easy? Tyler anchored one hand on the edge of the roof,
tensing his muscles so he could flip himself over.

A seagull screeched, wheeling past his face. Tyler took
his attention off El Gato for a split second. When he looked
back, the man had his weapon in his hand and was jumping
to the neighboring balcony.

Well, that's what he got for thinking this might have
been easy. Tyler swung down from the roof, eyed the gap
to the next balcony and followed.

The chilled champagne had come with the room. So
had the platter of chocolate-dipped strawberries and
the miniature pitcher of cream. It had all been meant to
stimulate the appetite, not satisfy it. Evidently the hotel
management assumed that a couple on their honeymoon
would be able to come up with all kinds of creative ways
to partake of the goodies.

But Emily hadn't been feeling very creative last night.
She'd just wanted to get drunk. She'd done a bang-up job
of it, too. No half measures for Emily Wright, no indeed,
because as she'd discovered, magnums of champagne
weren't meant to be consumed by one person.

Just like honeymoon suites weren't designed for single
occupancy.

She groaned and dropped her forehead against the
shower stall. The impact with the tiles started another turn
on the Tilt-A-Whirl that had set itself up inside her skull.
She groped for the faucets to turn off the water. Somehow,
they twisted the wrong way, cutting off the hot and opening
up the cold.

She cursed, jumped backward and promptly lost her

footing. She grabbed the faucets to keep from falling and managed to shut the cold. Meanwhile, the carnival ride picked up speed, morphing into a combination Ferris wheel and merry-go-round.

Emily pressed her fingers to her mouth and fought to keep down the contents of her stomach as she staggered out of the shower. She winced when she caught sight of herself in the mirror. Even soaking wet, her hair was starting to corkscrew. And she'd known she shouldn't have eaten the strawberries. The rash she got whenever she indulged was already mottling her chest and neck. But she'd wanted the chocolate, and besides, no one was here to see the rash. No one would see the black teddy she'd bought for her wedding night, or the red garter belt, either.

"Enough," she muttered, scowling at her reflection. "Pity party's over. Today is the first day of the rest of—"

Her voice broke before she could finish the trite phrase. Yet it was true. Her life stretched out in front of her, as full of possibilities —and as daunting—as a blank page. The only thing for certain was that Christopher wouldn't be part of it.

Fine. Good. So there was no reason to waste any more time mooning over what might have been, or the dreams that wouldn't come true. She was going to enjoy herself. She really was. She had paid for a full ten days before she had to return to reality.

A solitary reality.

"And that's good," she said, snatching up a towel. "Love is for fairy tales. And men are overrated." She was about to rub her hair dry when she thought better of it and gingerly blotted the water drops from the ends. "You don't need a man," she muttered. "You're tall enough to reach the top shelves in the cupboards. So aside from opening jars and scratching itches you can't reach, what are they good for? Besides totally screwing up your life?"

Buoyed by her pep talk, she walked to the bedroom. The sky glowed conch-shell pink through the glass above the louvered balcony doors. The overhead fan didn't do much to cut the mugginess; as first days went, this one promised to be a hot one. The sounds of dogs and seagulls, plus snatches of Spanish drifted from the plaza below. It was market day, she remembered. The brochure from the travel agency had featured pictures of it, but she wasn't sure she would be venturing outside until she felt more human. She dropped her towel beside the empty champagne bottle and rummaged through her suitcase for her underwear.

The first item she encountered was the red lace bra that went with the red garter belt. Why hadn't she repacked her luggage before she'd left?

For the same reason she hadn't canceled the honeymoon, she reminded herself, defiantly picking up the matching fire-engine-red panties. Because she'd wanted to prove she wasn't hurt. She might have indulged in pity for herself, but she'd be damned if she'd accept it from anyone else. Ten days would be plenty of time for her to lay the ghosts of all those happily-ever-after fantasies to rest. She would go back to Packenham Junction refreshed and tanned. That would show her family she was going to be just fine. Her coworkers at the paper would see that she was too tough to fall apart.

Only, they weren't her coworkers anymore. She'd worry about getting her job back once she got home. Actually, she would have to find a home first. She'd couldn't imagine going back to the apartment she'd shared with Christopher, but her options were limited. Her bank account was down to double digits, and she'd maxed out her credit cards to pay for this trip.

And all because she'd believed in a man. Put her faith in love. Opened her heart enough to buy into the whole pathetic fairy tale.

Emily crumpled the red lace in her hands and refused to acknowledge the moisture in her eyes. Damn. She wasn't going to cry. Not over him. She intended to enjoy this vacation, even if it killed her.

Something thumped on her balcony. She turned toward it just as a shadow moved across the louvers. An instant later the doors burst inward and crashed to the floor. A short, dark-haired man ran into the room. He was dressed like one of the construction workers in the square she'd noticed when she'd arrived yesterday, but even her alcohol-fogged brain didn't believe he'd entered her room by mistake. Construction workers didn't normally carry guns.

This couldn't really be happening, could it? Except for the gun, he looked as harmless as the guy who drove the milk truck to her parents' farm. Same round face and full lips, except there was a fine white scar across his chin and his eyes, instead of a merry brown, were black, and as dead as a snake's.

Emily's paralysis lasted no more than a heartbeat. A survival instinct she hadn't known she possessed took over and she reacted without thinking. "Get out!" she yelled, snapping her underwear at the intruder. "Out!" Her action appeared to startle him long enough to allow her to snatch the empty champagne bottle from the floor and swing it at his head.

He ducked, muttered something in Spanish and gave her a left jab that knocked her to the bed.

Both her stomach and the room wavered. She rolled to her feet on the other side of the mattress and was lifting the bottle to throw it at him when it shattered in her hand.

Shards of glass whizzed past her face and bounced on the sheets.

"Get down!" someone yelled from behind her.

Emily half turned in time to see another man lunge toward her from the balcony. He wrapped his arms around her legs and tackled her to the floor. She kicked and jabbed backward with her elbows. He quickly immobilized her by sliding up her body and folding one leg around hers.

There was a series of sharp pops. The lamp beside the bed exploded in a cloud of porcelain. The painting of the seascape on the wall crashed onto the platter on the room service cart, spraying leftover cream and strawberry hulls. Chunks of wood and plaster rained to the floor around her but none of it hit her. She couldn't move. She could hardly breathe. The second man was lying completely on top of her with his chin pressing down on her head. It felt as if he were built like a tree trunk.

As suddenly as they had started, the popping sounds halted. The door to the corridor banged open.

The weight on her back disappeared instantly. A pair of worn black cowboy boots moved into her vision. "Stay put," their owner ordered, vaulting over the bed. Footsteps pounded out of the room and down the corridor.

Emily hadn't meant to obey his command. Out of principle, she had vowed never to go along with what any man told her ever again.

But she was shaking so badly, she couldn't make her limbs work for a full minute. She lifted her head, gasping for breath. Her lungs filled with plaster dust. Coughing, she managed to get to her knees.

Through her tangled damp hair she saw the doors to the balcony were in splinters, their louvered slats strewn in ripples like broken fans. Pieces of dark green glass lay scattered over her bed, the clothes in her suitcase and even the towel she'd dropped on the floor. A line of small, round holes had appeared in the wall behind her.

Her brain struggled to process what she saw. Were those *bullet* holes? What on earth had happened here? Who were those men?

Belatedly, she thought of screaming but that might bring those men back.

She pushed herself to her feet, wobbled her way clear of the broken glass, and dashed for the room's door. She turned the lock, attached the chain, then leaned back against the panels and hugged her arms across her chest.

Only then did she realize that she was completely naked.

Her teeth started to chatter. She clamped her jaw and breathed hard through her nose. This was no time to panic. She was alive. That's what was important. So what if two strange maniacs had seen her naked? They obviously hadn't been here for *that* or they wouldn't have left. She had bigger concerns than modesty.

The door vibrated with a sharp knock. "Ma'am? Are you all right?"

Emily jumped away from the door. She recognized the voice, even though she'd heard him speak only four words. *Get down. Stay put.* It was the big man, the one who had tackled her. She ran back across the room and grabbed the phone.

The doorknob rattled. The man spoke again. "I'm sorry for frightening you, ma'am."

At home, the first speed-dial number on her phone was 911. Same with her cell phone, but she hadn't been able to get it to work here. She didn't think Rocama had 911 service anyway. And this phone was an old black rotary model. No push buttons or programmed numbers. She dialed the front desk.

A cheerful, female voice came through the phone, greeting her in Spanish.

Emily cupped her hand around the receiver. "I need the police," she said. "I've been attacked. I'm in room 307. The honeymoon suite. Please, help me."

There was a pause. *"No hablo inglés, señora. Momento, por favor."*

"Policía," Emily yelled. "Help me!" She got no response. She'd already been put on hold.

Something scraped outside her door. The lock clicked and it swung open to the limit of the chain. Emily watched, horrified, as the door kept moving. The bracket that held the chain slowly pulled out of the wall. A tall, blond man stepped over the threshold and nudged the door closed with his boot heel.

This was the man who had tackled her, all right. Those were the same worn black cowboy boots she'd seen beside her nose. A pair of jeans draped his long legs, a pale yellow golf shirt stretched across his broad shoulders and ropy muscles contoured his arms. His body looked just the way it had felt. Big, solid and very male. The only thing she hadn't been able to feel when he'd pinned her to the floor was the rifle that was slung over his back.

Finally, Emily did scream. She dropped the receiver and ran for the bathroom.

The blond man caught her from behind before she'd gone two steps. He slid one arm in front of her waist, lifted her from her feet and backed up so he could hang up the phone. Then he clamped his free hand over her mouth. "I'm not going to hurt you, but I can't let you call the police."

She twisted her head, trying to bite his hand, but he moved one finger under her chin to keep her jaw closed. She wriggled and kicked backward. One of her heels connected with his kneecap. Her elbow hit his ribs. And both her breasts rubbed and jiggled against his bare arms.

"Ma'am." His voice was strained. "This is not a good idea."

She could see that. Although his grip wasn't hurting her, it was solid enough to leave no doubt that he had her overpowered. Her struggle was getting her nowhere. It was only proving how strong he was. And how naked she was.

Oh, God. Maybe this was a nightmare and in another few seconds she would wake up in a heap of half-eaten strawberries and spilled champagne...

"No problem," he said. "It's under control."

Under control? Anger gave her a spurt of strength. She lifted her arms, aiming her nails at his face. He ducked his head behind hers, and she grabbed a handful of his hair instead. She yanked hard.

His grip didn't loosen. "Does anyone have him?"

She continued to flail as she tried to make sense of his question. He hadn't let go of her mouth, so he likely wasn't expecting an answer.

"White shirt, tan pants. No hard hat or tool belt. He left them on the first balcony."

It sounded as if he were describing the short man, the one who had struck her. But why? He didn't even seem to be talking to her.

"There was a civilian in the room. He opened fire. I lost him when I knocked her down." He spoke beside her ear. "Ma'am, are you hurt?"

What kind of criminal worried about the welfare of his victim? Or referred to her as a civilian? He was oddly calm about all this, too. As if he chased armed men through hotel rooms every day.

He had been *chasing* the guy who'd hit her. He'd tackled

her when the bullets had started flying. And so far he hadn't retaliated to any of her jabs or kicks, other than to restrain her. If he'd wanted to harm her, wouldn't he have done it by now?

It took a few seconds for the facts to click. It took a little longer than that for Emily to regain control over her body. She dropped her arms and went still.

He hesitated. "You're not hurt?"

She shook her head against his palm. "'m 'kay," she mumbled.

"I'm going to take my hand away from your mouth. Don't scream again."

She nodded an agreement. "'kay," she repeated.

Maintaining his hold on her waist with his other arm, he lifted his hand a scant half inch.

She inhaled as deeply as his grasp allowed. Which caused her breasts to rub across his arm again. She had to ignore it. He apparently was. Not that she had much there to keep a man's interest…

Focus! she ordered herself. This man might be able to overpower her physically, but he'd freed her mouth, and to Emily, words had always served as her best defense. "Who are you?" she demanded. "Are you a cop?"

"My name's Tyler Matheson."

"Who was that short man? Why were you chasing him?"

"That's confidential."

"You sound American. What's an American cop doing in Rocama? Why don't you want me to call the police?"

"It's for your own safety, ma'am." Still holding her suspended against the front of his body, he moved beside the bed. Then he pulled off the top sheet, gave it a flick to get rid of the bits of glass, and set Emily on her feet. "It's better if you don't get involved."

The ease with which he could sling her around was alarming. Panic tugged at her once more, but she fought it down. She had to use her head. That was easier said than done, considering the Tilt-A-Whirl still working away in there. "Who were you talking to before? Do you have a radio transmitter? Are you undercover or something?"

He draped the sheet around her shoulders and turned her to face him. "I'm sorry, ma'am. I'm not at liberty to answer your questions."

She spotted a coiled wire trailing from what looked like a receiver in his ear. He had to be law enforcement of some kind. She'd seen enough cops lately to recognize the discipline in his bearing.

But she'd never met a cop who looked like *this*. In spite of the conservative golf shirt, with those boots and jeans he looked more like a cowboy. His hair wasn't merely blond, it was sun-streaked and seemed permanently wind-tossed. His face had the lean, chiseled lines of someone who spent a lot of time looking into the distance. His eyes were dark blue. No, wait. There was a rim of brilliant cerulean around the irises. They only appeared dark because his pupils were dilated. His nostrils were flared, too, as if he were having as much difficulty drawing breath as she was. Her senses sharpened. She caught a whiff of lime aftershave and warm, male skin.

She fisted her hands in the sheet. Her pulse hadn't yet steadied, and now it accelerated again. It was probably the residual effects of the magnum of champagne, or maybe her brain was scrambled as a consequence of being knocked down, shot at and scared half out of her wits. Yet even with her limited mental faculties, she realized that Tyler Matheson was the sexiest-looking man she'd ever seen.

But a man, especially a handsome one, was the last

thing Emily Wright wanted to see right now. She'd flown a few thousand miles to escape the havoc wreaked by the last one.

Tyler wiped his palms on his pants. This woman was making him sweat worse than the tropical heat. She was only half a head shorter than he was, so their bodies had fit together as if they'd been made for each other. He could still feel the imprint of her breasts on his arm and her buttocks against his groin. How could any man be coherent in those circumstances?

But covering her with that sheet wasn't proving to be much of a help. The image of her going after El Gato armed with nothing but an empty bottle had been burned into his brain. Her freckled skin, her long legs, and her cloud of wet hair flying around her face… Damn, she'd been magnificent. Like a Valkyrie from one of the stories his Grandpa Lindstrom used to tell. Were there redheaded Valkyries?

"El Gato's spooked," Duncan said. "Unlikely he'll give us the chance to pick him out again in this crowd."

"Odds are he scrubbed the hit," Jack commented. "For today, anyway."

"Or he could be setting up along the route," Duncan said. "I'll give Lang and Gonzo an update. Meet you at the car, Jack."

"On my way now. What's the status of the civilian, junior?" Jack asked. "She need medical attention?"

Tyler forced himself to consider the woman objectively. He'd had a good look at every inch of her, and she hadn't appeared to have any injuries. He'd tried to cushion her as much as possible when he'd taken her to the floor. The redness that dotted the freckles above her breasts looked more like hives than rug burn. She hadn't moved as if she were hurt. She had a surprising amount of strength in her slender form, though she hadn't been able to wriggle free of his grip. Her attempts sure had made things interesting....

"Hey, Tyler?" Jack prodded. "You still there?"

He touched his fingertip to the red spot on the woman's cheek. "This needs ice. Do you have any other injuries?"

She shook her head, then winced as if she were in pain.

"Ma'am? Do you have a headache? Jack, she could have a concussion."

She freed one hand from the sheet and made an erasing motion. "It's not a concussion. I'm fine. Who are you talking to? How big an operation is this?"

He surveyed the room. It was in shambles. He spotted an overturned ice bucket near a dented room-service cart. Only a few wafers of ice remained. The rest had melted into a puddle beside a heap of red lace. He glanced at the king-size bed. Champagne. Sexy underwear. A naked woman. Someone appeared to have had a good time here the night before.

He'd assumed she was alone, since there was only one suitcase, and there was no sign of a man's clothes strewn around the room. He glanced at the open door to the bathroom. If whoever had shared the bed with her was still here, they wouldn't have let her fend for herself. He couldn't imagine a Valkyrie like her putting up with a coward. To be on the safe side, though, he went to check.

As he'd suspected, the bathroom was empty. It appeared only one of the towels had been used. If she'd had male company, he hadn't stayed the night. He grabbed a washcloth, returned to the puddle of melting ice and picked up a few of the larger pieces. He wrapped the ice in the washcloth and held it to her cheek. "This should keep the bruise from swelling."

She seemed startled by his action. But then she took the improvised ice pack from him and narrowed her eyes. "Who's going to clean up this mess? Your department better pay for the damage."

"We'll see to it."

"Who's 'we'?"

"Someone from the hotel will repair your doors."

"For all I know, the milkman shot up my suitcase. There could be bullet holes in my clothes. Are you going to pay for that, too?"

"Most of the shots hit the wall."

The woman moved the ice pack to her forehead. "You're ignoring my questions."

She was right about that. He saw no reason to reply, since her demands were probably an attempt at bravado. It was a common coping mechanism, and far easier for him to deal with than hysterics would have been.

Yet her questions weren't all he was trying to ignore. The sheet was gaping apart where she'd freed her arm, giving him a glimpse of shadowed skin. He didn't know why he found the view so compelling. He'd seen it all mere minutes ago.

"The major reported the ETA for the envoy's plane is fifty-five minutes," Duncan said. The background noise had changed from chickens to the sound of a revving engine. "Jack, where are you?"

"Here," Jack said. There was the sound of a car door slamming. "Junior, unless the civilian needs medical attention, you'd better wrap things up there and get over to the palace."

Tyler stepped backward. His heel came down on something soft. He suspected it was the red underwear.

"Look, Mr. Matheson or detective or whatever you are, I'd like some answers."

"Sorry, ma'am." He turned toward the door.

"And forget all the 'ma'ams.' I'm not in the best mood this morning. I'm not feeling exactly charitable toward men in general, either. You can't just burst into someone's room and then treat them like they don't exist." She dropped the ice pack, gathered the trailing edge of the sheet and followed him. "I'm thinking I shouldn't take your word that you'll pay for all this damage. Let me have your badge number."

"Ma'am, you'll have to trust me."

"Trust you? Right, sure. Like I'm going to trust anyone with a Y chromosome. Especially where money's concerned."

"Sounds as if she doesn't like you much, junior," Jack said.

"Maybe he needs reinforcements," Duncan said.

"Maybe he's flirting."

"Then he does need help. Anyone give him the birds and bees talk?"

"Nah. I thought we should wait until the boy hits puberty."

No one could mistake Tyler for a boy. He had just turned thirty, and at six foot four and two hundred and fifteen pounds, he was the largest man in Eagle Squadron. But he was also the newest, so he'd been subjected to this kind of razzing for nearly a year. It was hard to overcome his status as a rookie with a team this tight. "Give it a rest," he muttered.

The woman's face went red. "Me? Give it a rest? I—"

"No, not you," Tyler said. He turned his head and pointed to the receiver in his ear. "Party line."

"Okay, then let me speak to your supervisor."

He reached for the doorknob. "Sorry. No time."

"Right, just like a man." She grasped his arm. "You've got enough time to screw up my life but then you waltz out without footing the bill. Not this time, buster. I want to see a badge right now or I'm phoning the Rocaman police."

This was more than bravado. There was genuine anger here. She hadn't known him long enough to dislike him this much, so she must be thinking of someone else. He looked at her hand. She wore no jewelry, yet there was a band of pale skin at the base of her ring finger. Was it from a wedding band? Had she come to Rocama to celebrate her divorce? Or to cheat on her husband? Whatever her story, her touch on his skin felt good. Almost as good as when her breast had rubbed over that spot...

Yet again, he jerked his attention back to business. He sorted through what she'd said. "You called him the milkman."

"What?"

"The man I was chasing."

"So what if I did?"

"Why?"

"He reminded me of someone."

Tyler let go of the doorknob and put his hand over hers. "Then you got a good look at him?"

"He was hard to ignore." She moved her jaw from side to side. "I got a good, close-up look at his fist, too."

"Would you recognize him if you saw him again?"

She nodded. "I never forget a face."

"Hold it, junior," Jack said. "If she can identify El Gato..."

Tyler had already turned and was leading her back across the room. "I'm way ahead of you, Doc."

Halfway there, she yanked free. "Look, cowboy, it's bad enough that you're carrying on a conversation with people who aren't here instead of answering my questions. If you need me to testify or something, that's fine, as long as it doesn't cut into my vacation. But that doesn't mean you can haul me around like a sack of last year's potatoes."

"Sorry, ma'am. I'm in a hurry." He picked up her suitcase and emptied it on the bed.

"What are you doing?" she demanded.

"Finding you some clothes." He pushed aside a pile of silk and lace. Hadn't she packed anything besides underwear? From the looks of her wardrobe, she'd been planning to spend most of her stay in Rocama in her hotel room.

But he couldn't allow himself to be curious about her any more than he could acknowledge the warmth he still felt on his arm from her touch. He spotted what looked like a dress, or at least something with more fabric than the rest of her garments. Unfortunately, it had a neat, round, thirty-caliber hole in the bottom. He tossed it to her anyway. "This is a matter of national security, ma'am. You're going to have to come with me."

Chapter 2

Tyler Matheson wasn't a cop. He was a soldier. Emily decided to believe that much of his story, since the man who claimed to be his commanding officer was wearing what had to be a genuine army uniform. An impressive array of ribbons and medals decorated Major Mitchell Redinger's chest, and the shine on his shoes would put a mirror to shame.

Yet even if the major had been in blue jeans and a golf shirt like Sergeant Matheson, he couldn't have been mistaken for anything else. His dark hair was cut military-short, he kept his back and shoulders military-straight and he radiated the quiet confidence of a natural leader. In fact, with his granite jaw and the distinguished touch of silver at his temples, he was so army that he could have posed for a recruiting poster.

Fine. Good. Emily could accept that they were American soldiers, but the rest was more difficult to absorb. If it wasn't for the bruise on her jaw and the persistent hangover that throbbed at the base of her skull, she might be tempted to suspect she was still back in her hotel in a champagne-induced coma. This kind of thing just didn't happen to people from Packenham Junction.

They were meeting the major in the family wing of the governor's palace. According to her travel brochure, the three-story structure was centuries old and a showpiece of Spanish Colonial architecture. There were guided tours of the public areas like the grand ballroom and the reception hall, but this area was off-limits to tourists. Not that she'd had the chance to sightsee as Tyler had rushed her through a side door and down a portrait gallery. Still, this room he'd brought her to was breathtaking enough. It was all dark wood beams, pale peach-tinted plaster and floors of glazed terra-cotta tile. Lush bouquets of tropical flowers rested on delicate, gilded tables. A long couch and several chairs upholstered in ivory brocade were grouped in the center of the floor.

But the major hadn't asked her to sit. He obviously hadn't expected this interview to last long. Tyler hadn't gotten comfortable, either. He had taken up a post beside the potted ferns that flanked the doors, his feet braced apart and his hands clasped behind his back. Though he wasn't looking at her, Emily had the feeling he was fully aware of everything she did.

On the other hand, just because she was conscious of everything *he* did didn't mean the interest was mutual. Not that she was interested. The sooner she could be rid of him, the better. She'd never had much tolerance for take-charge men, no matter how sexy they happened to be.

She slid the strap of her sundress back on her shoulder and crossed her arms. "El Gato?"

"It's what the assassin is known as," the major replied.

"And you really don't know what he looks like?"

"We have only general descriptions."

"How is that possible? With the number of surveillance cameras around nowadays, I would have thought he'd have been photographed by now."

"Not at a crime scene."

"What about his passport?"

"He would have several passports in different names, and in all probability, he's been filmed by airport security innumerable times, but that doesn't allow us to track him. Surveillance footage of crowds is useless unless Intelligence knows what he looks like in the first place."

"There must have been someone else who could identify him."

"Miss Wright, the main reason no one can identify this criminal is because it's his practice to leave no witnesses. The body of a young construction worker was found three blocks from the plaza an hour ago. He had been stripped and strangled."

She remembered the casual way El Gato had struck her. And the bullet holes in her hotel room wall at the height of her head. If it hadn't been for Tyler...

She hugged her arms more tightly across her chest. "So he's dangerous. But since when does the United States Army concern itself with catching criminals? We're not even on American soil. What about Interpol? Or the Rocaman Police? From what the cowboy told me—" she lifted one hand to gesture toward Tyler "—this sounds like a job for cops, not soldiers."

"We aren't concerned with apprehending El Gato," the major said. "We want only to stop him."

"That still doesn't answer my question."

"El Gato's target is an American citizen, specifically our envoy to Rocama. Our mission is to protect the envoy."

"You're acting as bodyguards? Is that what you're telling me?"

"Essentially, yes."

"All right, then why don't you just stick the envoy in a bulletproof Humvee and put a bunch of sharpshooters in helicopters? Why all this secrecy? Don't you trust the Rocamans?"

A faint buzzer sounded before Major Redinger could reply. He took a cell phone from his pocket, listened briefly, then snapped it shut. "Miss Wright, the envoy is due to arrive at the palace within the hour. Can we count on your cooperation?"

"I already told Sergeant Matheson I'd be willing to testify if there's a trial. I know how that works. Or do you want me to talk with a sketch artist or something, so you know who you're looking for?"

"While I appreciate the offer, I'm afraid time is of the essence. We need a more hands-on approach." He nodded to Tyler, who immediately turned from the window and came forward. "We'd like you to accompany Sergeant Matheson as he continues his surveillance of the plaza."

"What? You're kidding."

"This is not a laughing matter, Miss Wright. We want you to point out El Gato if you see him."

"Now, wait a minute," she said, backing up. "I only agreed to meet with you because I wanted some guarantee that the damage to my room and my belongings will be covered. That's all. I've got plans for today."

Redinger glanced at Tyler. "Sergeant?"

"I already assured Miss Wright we'd take care of the damage, Major."

"Then what's the problem?"

"Miss Wright doesn't trust anyone with a Y chromosome, sir."

Emily bumped into a side table. She turned to steady the vase of flowers it held. And to hide the blush that was burning her cheeks. Had she said that? Probably. But the way Tyler had repeated her words in a flat, impersonal tone, as if he were making an official report, had made them sound petty. Bitter. As if she were so focused on her grudge against the male sex that she couldn't see there were more important things happening in the world. Things that didn't revolve around her and her hurt feelings.

Yes, well, maybe she was indulging herself a little too much with that. He might understand where she was coming from if he'd had his life turned upside down and stomped on, too. It was the morning after what should have been her wedding night. Her wounds were too fresh for her to feel reasonable. She was entitled to some anger.

It was preferable to tears.

She stopped fidgeting with the vase and lifted her chin. "I'm here for a vacation. A nice, relaxing, stress-free ho—" She swallowed. She had almost said honeymoon. "Holiday," she finished.

"Not anymore," the major said.

"What do you mean?"

"Miss Wright, you must understand the seriousness of the situation. If we know you can identify El Gato, then it's certain that he has reached the same conclusion. He will likely decide to silence you."

"What? No, he couldn't know I remember him. Most people wouldn't. It happened really fast. I just have a knack for faces."

"We have no doubt he's responsible for the death of the construction worker today. That's his pattern. You can't resume your vacation as if nothing has happened. He knows where you're staying, and he's already tried to kill you once."

Was the major deliberately trying to scare her? He didn't appear to be. His matter-of-fact manner hadn't changed. Neither had the quiet confidence he projected. And that made what he was saying all the more scary.

"If you choose to work with us, we can keep you safe. But if you don't, then your only alternative is to leave Rocama City immediately."

"No way. I'm not going home yet. I couldn't. I just got here. I already paid for ten days."

Major Redinger dipped his chin in a tight nod. "You made the best choice, Miss Wright. Our government is grateful for your help."

"Wait. I didn't say—"

"Sergeant Matheson?"

"Yes, sir?"

"Time to get into position."

Tyler saluted the major, took Emily's elbow and turned her toward the doorway. "This way, ma'am."

They were in the gallery and had passed by the first three portraits before she had the presence of mind to wrench her arm free. This wasn't the first time he'd hauled her around like this. Why did she keep letting him get away with it?

He walked ahead without slowing

"What just happened in there?" she called after him. "I didn't agree to anything."

"You volunteered."

"No, I didn't."

"It's all the same in the army."

"I'm not *in* the army. I'm an American citizen on vacation. You can't just…draft me. All I said was that I wasn't going to turn tail and run."

"Right, Valkyries don't."

The echo from the tile floor must have distorted his

words. She jogged to catch up to him. "What did you say?"

"We'll be watching from an outdoor café that's to the east of the palace. We'll keep a wall and the sun to our backs so you'll be safe. From there we'll have a good view of the plaza and the approach to the palace gates."

"You said something that sounded like Valkyrie. What was it?"

"I don't recall."

"You don't like answering questions much, do you?"

"No. Once we're in position, I'll be watching the higher vantage points, since I know what El Gato looks like from a distance. You can scan the faces of the people in the plaza. Pay particular attention to those near the palace's public entrance. There's no time to fit you with a com device, but I'll pass along what you say through mine, so sing out if you spot anyone familiar."

"It sounds too simple."

"The best solutions usually are." He pushed open one of the double doors at the end of the corridor, looked outside, then gestured for her to exit first. A shady courtyard paved with cobblestones stretched in front of them. "Ready?"

"Would it make any difference if I said I wasn't?"

"Would it make any difference if I told you the envoy's a woman?"

She scowled as she stepped outside. "No, why should it?"

He shrugged. "I thought you might be more inclined to save a life if you knew it wasn't male."

Given the parameters of the mission, the team had decided ahead of time that going low-profile was the best strategy, which was why the convoy from the airport consisted of only two vehicles. They would be hiding the envoy in plain sight, so they depended on blending in with the rest of the traffic. On the surface, there was nothing remarkable about the cars they were using, yet they were unlike anything the locals would be driving.

Each was equipped with a transponder that enabled their positions to be tracked to within a few meters. Major Redinger and Chief Warrant Officer Esposito were monitoring their communications and GPS coordinates from the operations base they'd set up at the palace. Among other special features, the cars had run-flat tires and a supply of smoke bombs in case a quick escape was called for. Their biggest advantage was the fact that Kurt Lang was driving the car that carried the envoy. He had a spooky affinity for anything mechanized.

Tyler's earbud crackled to life. "Entering the Old Quarter now," Lang said. "We should be at the gates in twenty."

"How's it look at that end, junior?" Duncan asked. He and Jack were in the lead car. While they would be alert for choke points and possible ambushes, their main purpose was to find the optimum route to keep their small convoy moving.

Tyler balanced his chair on its back legs and continued the methodical survey he'd been doing for the past quarter hour. He scrutinized the buildings around the plaza, concentrating on the roofs first and then on the facades. It was approaching noon, so much of the activity in the marketplace at the south end of the plaza had tapered off. He activated his transmitter. "Still clear."

"What about our witness?"

He reached across the round café table to touch Emily's arm. "Ma'am?"

She tipped down her sunglasses and looked at him over the rims. "If you're asking me whether I see the guy, the answer is still no. I told you that I'll tell you if I do, so trust me on that. I have absolutely no reason to keep that information to myself, since according to your major, the guy might decide to use me for target practice."

Someone snickered. "A bit tetchy today, isn't she?" Lang commented.

"Guess she doesn't like babysitting junior," Jack said.

"Can you blame her? The smell of his acne cream alone makes most women run."

"Enough chatter, people," Redinger cut in. "Let's keep this channel clear for business."

Emily poked her finger against Tyler's forearm. "What happens if I do spot him? Are you going to shoot him?"

He switched off his mike. "Ma'am—"

"Where's that big gun you had? I don't see it."

He'd left his sniper rifle at the palace, but Tyler was seldom unarmed. At the moment he had a laser-sighted pistol concealed at the small of his back, four spare ammo magazines in his pockets, an extra pistol strapped to his left calf and his favorite knife in his right boot. "A weapon like that tends to attract attention in a sidewalk café," he said. "How's your orange juice, ma'am?"

"You're changing the subject."

"Yes."

"Fine. The juice is nice and cold. But I would have preferred coffee."

"Orange juice is better for a hangover."

She parted her lips as if she were about to argue, then sighed and picked up her glass. "How did you guess?"

He slanted her a glance. "Empty booze bottle, ice pack on forehead, bloodshot eyes." He didn't mention her foul mood. He suspected that had started before she'd overindulged.

"You're observant."

"I'm trained to be."

"Then if you're that observant, why weren't you able to see El Gato's face yourself?"

"I only saw him from above and from behind. Then I was focused on getting you out of the line of fire."

She took a long swallow of juice. "I should thank you. You probably saved my life."

"You're welcome, ma'am."

"But you wouldn't have needed to save my life in the first place if you hadn't chosen my balcony window to crash through."

It had been this way since they'd sat down. Emily seemed to like to talk, yet for every civil comment she made, she tacked on something argumentative. She had to realize he hadn't chosen her window. He'd been following El Gato. "It won't work," Tyler said.

"What?"

"I'm not going to quarrel with you."

"I don't know what—"

"I grew up with four sisters. I can tell when a woman is trying to pick a fight."

She set her glass down on the table with a clunk.

"The man you're really angry with," Tyler said. "Is he your husband?"

"I'm not married."

"Divorced, then?"

"Why would you think that I should be either? Women don't need men to complete them, you know. It's not as if marriage is the be-all and end-all of our existence. It's incredibly chauvinistic of you to assume—"

"Whoa, I didn't assume anything." He gestured to her hand. "You've got a tan line on your ring finger, that's all."

She pushed her sunglasses back into place and crossed

her arms, tucking her left hand beneath her elbow. "It's none of your business."

"It is if your attitude toward men is going to interfere with your ability to help us."

For a change, she remained silent.

Tyler took the time to study her. The strap of her dress slid off her shoulder again. It had been doing that since they'd left her hotel room. Hadn't she packed anything that wasn't designed for seduction? Without the support of the strap, her scoop neckline gaped enough to show a hint of cleavage. He suspected she wouldn't have had cleavage if not for her tightly crossed arms. Not that her breasts were too small. They would fit perfectly in his palms.

Emily couldn't be called classically beautiful. Her chin was pointed and she kept it thrust out. Her long, narrow nose was covered with freckles, as was most of her skin that was visible. Her most striking feature, her vivid green eyes, were hidden behind the dark lenses of her sunglasses. As for her mouth, she was effectively hiding that behind a tight-lipped expression, so he had no idea how she normally looked. She'd tried to tame her hair into a ponytail with a fabric-covered elastic, but big chunks of it had escaped to hang in wild, red curls against her nape and her cheeks. The curls looked wiry, yet he suspected they would be soft to the touch. He imagined winding a lock around his finger. Or maybe spreading it across a pillow.

A man could get lost in all that hair. Considering the energy she was putting into her anger, she'd be something else if she ever channeled that into passion.

She drummed her fingers on her arm. "If you don't like my attitude, that's too bad. I didn't ask to be here. I was hijacked. Or press-ganged. Or whatever it is you people do to civilians."

"You're free to leave."

"Right. Then I'd never see the money for the damage to my hotel room." She fingered the hem of her dress. "Not to mention my clothes. Did you know there's a bullet hole in my dress?"

"You can trust—"

"Hah. We've already had this conversation, so you know what I think about the issue of trust. Whether you're a soldier or not, you're still a man."

Tyler started another scan of the plaza. He waited until he was done before he spoke again. "He really did a number on you, didn't he?"

"Who?"

"The guy whose ring you wore."

"Okay, Mr. Observant," she snapped. "You're right. I'm pissed off at one particular scuzzball, and I'm taking it out on the gender at large. Why do you think I needed this vacation?" She picked up her glass again and drained it, then slipped her fingers beneath her sunglasses and wiped her eyes.

He kept his face impassive. Emily probably didn't realize that he could see her on the edge of his vision. Otherwise, she wouldn't have given herself away by wiping her tears. She wouldn't have realized that he could hear the catch in her breathing, either, that telltale, hiccupping gasp that women made when they were trying not to cry. Emily wouldn't want him to know there was any softness under the prickly hide she armored herself with.

So he resisted the sudden urge he felt to pull her into his arms. He knew instinctively that she wouldn't welcome the offer of a shoulder to cry on. She had too much pride to accept sympathy from a stranger. And that's what they were. Strangers. In spite of the fact that he'd seen and felt her naked body…and that he was imagining what he'd do if he had that opportunity again.

He brought the front legs of his chair to the ground with a thud. The mission was his priority. He couldn't let Emily's feelings interfere with it any more than he could let his own. "You're not crying, are you, ma'am?"

"Of course not. I'm just rubbing my bloodshot, hungover eyes."

"Ah."

"Crying is for dainty little ladies who lie around on fainting couches and wave their lace hankies at their maids. And in case you haven't noticed, I'm neither dainty nor little. I don't own a lace hanky. So I assure you, I never cry."

"Good."

She sniffed. "You're like every other guy, aren't you? You claim you can't stand to see a woman cry. You don't mind making them cry, but once you drive them to it you go all helpless and brain-dead and run the other way."

"My only concern is the mission."

"So why pretend that you care whether or not I was crying?"

"Because if your vision is blurry, you wouldn't be able to see El Gato."

She turned to stare at him.

Tyler continued to watch the plaza. He steeled himself for another rant. Instead, she did something completely unexpected. She laughed.

It was a wonderful laugh. Rich and uninhibited, even if it was partly at her own expense. She was letting him glimpse the woman beneath the prickly hide, and he wanted to see more of her. He wished now that he could have pulled her into his arms. Not simply to feel her body against his again, but to feel *her.*

Her laughter tapered off. She shook her head, then sucked in her breath, stilled quickly and pressed her palm against her forehead. "Well, Sergeant Tyler Matheson," she said, "even though you're a man, you've got one thing in your favor."

"What?"

"When you decide to use a woman, at least you're honest about it."

There was no safe response he could make to that, so Tyler fell back on the classic male reply. He grunted.

Emily propped her elbows on the table and rested her chin on her hands. A tour group was heading across the plaza from her hotel. They were making slow progress, since a few of them were stopping to haggle with the marketplace vendors. There weren't many left. One of the farmers sold his final bunch of bananas and started pushing his wheelbarrow away. She watched him for a while to ensure he wasn't El Gato, then shifted her concentration to the tour group.

With the exception of the guide, who was a young Hispanic woman, everyone had white hair and varying shades of sunburns. The only male among them was close to six feet tall and as thin as a rail.

If things had gone differently this morning, she might have been on that tour. She'd seen an advertisement for it in the hotel lobby. They would be following a walking route that would touch on the main attractions of the Old City, beginning with the Governor's Palace. But they wouldn't be able to go into the family wing where she'd been, or to see what she had. The tourists looked uncomfortably hot out in the sun, too. Although she wasn't about to admit it to Tyler, being on this stakeout wasn't entirely unpleasant. The table he had chosen in this café was in the shade, and a breeze had come up that relieved the humidity. She could smell the tang of the sea, as well as a heady mix of flowers and citrus fruit. Or was that Tyler's lime aftershave?

It was interesting that in spite of his finger-combing approach to styling his hair, he'd taken the time to shave before he'd gone out tracking assassins this morning. Perhaps he limited himself to one grooming task a day. Shaving a face like his couldn't have been easy to accomplish without nicks, given the squareness of his jaw and the depth of the creases that framed his mouth. His chin had the hint of a cleft, too. She wondered whether she'd feel a trace of beard stubble if she pressed her thumb to the center of the cleft, or maybe trailed her fingertips along those dramatic hollows beneath his cheekbones.

She shifted her chair farther away from his. It didn't help. She was still more aware of him than she wanted to be. Which was understandable, since there was so much of him.

He had to be at least six foot three, maybe four. From what she could see of his arms, there didn't appear to be an ounce of fat on him. His muscles were taut and well-defined. A haze of dark blond hair softened the contours of his forearms and the backs of his hands. She'd already felt how strong his grip was, yet his fingers were slender. Long. Supple. She imagined they would be gentle if he stroked her instead of grasped.

She gritted her teeth as her body reacted to the memory of his touch. It had been adrenaline, she reminded herself, not attraction. The idea that she could be attracted to any man right now was absurd. Like a burn victim ripping off the bandages from her fingers because she couldn't wait to play with matches again.

Emily searched for something caustic to say to reinforce the distance between them. It had been working for her so far.

Yet nothing came. It was tough to hang on to her anger. Especially when Tyler remained so calm. He was dealing with her words the same way he'd dealt with the blows she'd given him in her hotel room. Instead of retaliating, he let her flail until she realized that she wasn't getting anywhere.

He must have frustrated the hell out of his sisters.

"Affirmative," he said. "Still clear, Miss Wright?"

He'd been checking in regularly with his team, so she was getting accustomed to his one-sided conversations. She nodded. "I don't see him."

He said a few more words, then tapped his finger against his shirt near the side of his waist. It's where she assumed the control for his microphone was located.

A silence fell between them. It wasn't what she'd call companionable. More like a temporary cease-fire. The breeze stirred her hair. She gathered what had come loose, lifted it off her neck and redid her ponytail. "How much longer now?" she asked.

"You should see the lead car any minute."

She looked past the market stalls to the west side of the plaza where a narrow road emerged from between the hotel and the courthouse. She would have had a good view of it from her hotel balcony.

Which was why the assassin had been there. He would have had a clear shot at the car carrying the envoy. While Emily had been stumbling around in the shower and venting her grievances with men, a killer had cold-bloodedly been preparing to end someone's life. Reminding herself of that fact did help put her own troubles into perspective.

"Don't worry," Tyler said. "We're almost done."

Of course, he'd think she was anxious to be finished with this task. She'd done nothing but complain about it. She cleared her throat. "About what you said earlier…"

"When?"

"Before we left the palace. You made a crack about me wanting to save a life if the person was female. I just need you to know that I wouldn't like to see anyone hurt, male or female."

The corners of his mouth softened. It wasn't a smile, only the promise of one. "I figured that, or you would have left by now."

"I do want to help you stop this guy. I was just feeling cranky enough to give you a hard time."

"No problem. I could see you were only blowing off steam."

"Your sisters taught you well."

"Yeah. How's your headache?"

"It's getting better."

"Good."

The breeze stirred another whiff of his aftershave. She searched for something else to distract her. "This envoy you're protecting. What's her name?"

He paused, as if weighing how much to tell her. "Helen Haggerty."

"Haggerty," she repeated. "Any relation to General Haggerty, hero of Desert Storm?"

"He was her father."

"Ah, now I get it."

"Get what?"

"That's why the army was sent to play bodyguard. Because she's Hurricane Haggerty's daughter."

He grunted.

"But I still don't get why you're using these cloak-and-dagger tactics. Unless you really don't trust the local authorities." She tipped her head toward a pair of policemen in dark blue uniforms who were walking past the palace gates. "Is that it?"

"I just follow orders, ma'am."

"This visit from the envoy must be really important. What's going on? Why does someone want to kill her?"

"You ask a lot of questions."

"It's an occupational hazard."

"What do you do for a living?" he asked.

"I'm between jobs right now, as they say, thanks to the scuzzball. That's one of the reasons the money issue is so important to me. You might think it's petty for me to worry about that, considering the serious stuff going on here, but I don't have extra to pay for room repairs or new clothes. Once I get back to the States I'll need to…" She trailed off.

Tyler leaned toward her. "Did you see something?"

She shook her head. Another chunk of hair sprang out of her ponytail but she ignored it. If she wasn't afraid of rekindling her headache, she'd be tempted to smack herself in the forehead.

Because of Christopher, she didn't want to trust any man. Her knee-jerk reaction to anything a male said or did was to resist. She'd been picking fights with Tyler out of principle. She'd been too busy nursing her temper and feeling sorry for herself to think of the big picture. Or to see what was right under her nose.

Yes, she was unemployed, but she'd always regarded her job at the *Packenham Observer* as temporary. That was why Christopher had talked her out of it so easily. She'd wanted to do something better, something more challenging. More…important.

Like a story about a clandestine military operation to stop an international assassin?

Her pulse did a fluttering hop, then accelerated into a flat-out run. The last remnants of fog cleared from her brain, as if she'd suddenly awakened. Or more to the point, sobered up.

Good God! Why hadn't she seen this sooner? What Tyler had brought her into was as far removed from accounts of town council meetings and county fairs as she could get. Until now, her most exciting story had been an exposé of the faulty radar gun that was churning out a profit for the local speed trap.

This wasn't an infringement on her vacation. It was a once-in-a-lifetime opportunity. It could open doors for her at every major paper in the Midwest. Instead of being unemployed when she got home, she could have a story to peddle that would kick-start her career.

She yanked off her sunglasses and looked at Tyler. So far, neither he nor Major Redinger had been willing to answer her questions. That was going to change.

"You're sure you don't notice anything?" he asked.

She leaned closer until she could see the rim of cerulean around his irises. "You're using me."

"What?"

"It's okay. You already admitted it. You need my help."

"Where are you going with this?"

"Establishing the ground rules. You're using me, so I'm going to use you." She reached forward, intending to press her index finger against the spot near his waist.

He caught her hand. "What are you doing?"

"How do you turn on your mic?"

"Why?"

"I want to say something to Major Redinger."

He pinned her hand flat to the table beneath his. "Say it to me."

It was hard to think clearly when he was this close. She tried breathing through her mouth so she wasn't quite so conscious of his scent. "I'm willing to cooperate with you and your team for as long as you need me. In return, I want your guarantee that you'll give me an exclusive on this story."

"What story?"

For the first time since she'd thrown Christopher's ring down his garbage chute, Emily actually smiled. "That, Sergeant Matheson, is what I intend to find out."

Chapter 3

Tyler reached the top of the stairs, pushed aside a sheet of plastic and ducked his head beneath the low door frame that led to the servants' quarters. The restoration work in this area of the Governor's Palace had been suspended in order to provide Eagle Squadron with an operations base for the duration of their mission in Rocama. The location was ideal, since the back staircases that had been designed for the servants' use gave the team ready access to both the floor that held the room assigned to the envoy and the courtyard at the heart of the palace complex. The low ceilings, the crumbling plaster on the walls and the stacks of paint cans in a few of the corners didn't bother anyone. As field headquarters went, the conditions were downright luxurious.

Tyler followed the sound of voices to the room he was sharing with Jack and Duncan. Kurt and Gonzo were presently shadowing the envoy and would stay with her until she was settled in her suite. The group of palace guards who would take over from there had been handpicked by the Rocaman president and had also been screened by Duncan's pals back at Intelligence. There was no question of their loyalty. The rest of the team would be relaxing while they could.

"I'll give you five to one odds the major won't go for it," Jack said, shucking off his vest. He laced his fingers together and stretched his arms over his head until his back popped.

"No bet, Doc." Duncan withdrew the spare magazines from his pockets and returned them to the stack in the steel ammo box. "We all know Redinger's not going to agree."

Tyler emptied his own pockets, adding to the stack of ammunition. "Emily can be persistent."

Duncan chuckled. "That's one way to put it."

"Hey, junior," Jack said. "You still got both ears? Sure she didn't chew one off?"

"I've got no problem with my hearing, Doc. You're confusing me with senior citizens like you."

"But jeez, a reporter," Jack persisted. "Why couldn't you crash in on a Mob accountant or maybe a mime? Someone who knows how to keep quiet?"

Tyler had been thinking along the same lines himself. A reporter. He should have guessed, considering how many questions Emily liked to ask. She had an ease with language that was exceptional, even for a woman. She seemed naturally curious, as well as determined, two qualities that would be useful to a journalist.

But she was bound to be disappointed. Duncan was right. The major would never allow her to publish any story about this mission, no matter how much she argued. It wasn't merely an issue of national security, it was a matter of their personal safety. Eagle Squadron relied on remaining anonymous. They operated under the radar. Most of their missions were accomplished before anyone realized they'd been there.

Still, part of him would be sorry to see the last of her. Emily was stimulating company. He was coming to enjoy her banter. It was evidence of her quick mind. He wondered what her ex-husband had done to make her so angry. Or maybe he had been a fiancé. Whoever had given her the ring she'd worn, Tyler had little doubt that she'd been the one to break off the relationship. He couldn't imagine any man willingly letting a spitfire like her go.

"Funny you should mention quiet, Doc," Tyler said, "considering that female you were in charge of on the mission last fall."

Jack grinned. "Which one do you mean? As I recall, there were two."

"The little one with the good lungs."

Duncan tapped the side of his head. "Yeah, my ears have been ringing since we got back. That kid could shatter glass."

Jack went to his duffel bag and pulled out a small digital camera. "That reminds me. The pipsqueak got another tooth. Want to see the pictures?"

Duncan groaned while Tyler laughed. "Have mercy. No more. Please."

"Eva bought her this teething ring you can fill with cold water," Jack said, turning the camera display toward them. "See? It helps, but what the kid really needs is a steak."

"Now I know why Kurt and Gonzo wanted to take the first shift," Duncan said.

Jack had clicked through at least two dozen photos of his fiancée's daughter and her new tooth when Chief Warrant Officer Esposito stuck his head into the room.

Light gleamed from his bald pate. "The major wants to see you, Matheson."

Tyler's smile vanished. He wasn't looking forward to this. The guys had merely razzed him about involving a journalist, but they'd known it had just been back luck. It could have happened to any of them. The major, however, wouldn't see any humor in the situation. Though Mitchell Redinger had been known to bend the rules occasionally for the sake of his men, he rarely loosened up. He lived and breathed the job.

Tyler went down the hall to a room that smelled heavily of fresh paint. It was larger than the others so it was being used as the communications and briefing room. Esposito settled on a stool in front of a shelf of electronic equipment. Redinger was leaning over a square table, his hands braced on either side of what appeared to be a blueprint of the palace. He waved Tyler forward. "There's a small bedroom on the same floor as the suite assigned to the envoy. It has no phone, and the closest access to the outside is through the stairwell that we're already monitoring. We've put her in there."

"Ms. Haggerty?"

"No, Emily Wright."

"I don't understand, sir."

Redinger straightened and the blueprint rolled shut. "It should keep her out of the way."

Tyler cleared his throat. "I'm not sure that confining her will work, Major."

"Confining her?"

"She's a resourceful woman, and she would resist any attempt to restrict her movements."

"I noticed. She's also very astute. She's already put more pieces together concerning this mission than she should have. That could present a serious problem unless we take measures immediately."

"I realize that we can't give Miss Wright what she wants, but I don't believe she would present a security risk. She's intelligent enough to understand the harm she could do by publicizing our activities."

"She not only understands the harm, she understands that she has a powerful bargaining chip because of it."

"Imprisoning her won't win her cooperation."

Redinger lifted one eyebrow. "You misunderstood, Sergeant. We're not imprisoning her, we're embedding her."

"Sir?"

"Apart from her separate sleeping quarters, she will be participating in all our daily activities."

Tyler had difficulty grasping what he was hearing. He and the rest of the team trusted Redinger with their lives. After decades of operating in secrecy, he couldn't be taking Eagle Squadron public, could he?

"You seem confused, Matheson. Weren't you aware of the deal Miss Wright proposed?"

"Yes, Major. She would continue to assist us in identifying El Gato as long as we allowed her to gather material for an article on us and on our mission here. But I hadn't expected you to agree."

"It was the best option. Otherwise, she might not only refuse to help us, she could attempt to go to the media immediately, which would cause us to divert our resources at a critical time. She also doesn't appear to comprehend the risk to her personal safety if she remains in Rocama on her own."

That sounded like Emily, all right.

"We don't want her to be a target any more than we want her to be a loose cannon," the major went on. "That's why it's imperative that we maintain control. By embedding her, we do exactly that."

This still wasn't making sense. Allowing Emily to be an embedded journalist would only delay the publicity. It would keep her safe and save this mission, but what about the next one? What about Eagle Squadron's future?

The major picked up the rolled print and stored it on the equipment shelf. "For the duration of the envoy's visit, Miss Wright will remain where we can monitor her activities and her communications. That's where you come in."

"Major?"

"Her safety will be your responsibility."

"What about my duties?"

"You'll need to incorporate her into them so she can help us identify El Gato."

"She'll expect to interview us."

"I trust you to use your judgment concerning how much to say. The less you give her, the less we need to worry about afterward. Avoid discussing past missions or anything classified but give her enough to keep her occupied. Giving personal details would present the lowest risk. As long as she believes she'll get what she wants in the end, it's in her best interest to cooperate."

Understanding flooded him all at once. He should have realized it immediately. The major would agree to Emily's deal because it was expedient. He would do whatever was necessary for the success of a mission, just as he'd trained the rest of them to do. That didn't mean he was going to follow through on his promise. "Once the mission is over, you're not going to let her story get published."

"Correct. That's out of the question. We can't compromise Eagle Squadron's anonymity."

"But how—"

"We'll do a full cleanup before we leave."

Tyler knew what the major meant. They'd done it before when they'd needed to eliminate any trace of their presence. In addition to removing all physical evidence, the team would need to destroy Emily's notes and any photographs she might have taken. They would deny they had ever been in Rocama. If she did attempt to publish an account of them, even without any documentation, there were other, more heavy-handed legal measures the major could take. When it came to national security, the government had a long and powerful reach.

His conscience stirred. "Is it necessary to deceive her? Maybe it would help if we explained the need for confidentiality more thoroughly."

"I tried, Sergeant. I don't like deceiving her, either, but she wasn't in what I'd call a reasonable frame of mind."

"She's having a rough time. She's recovering from some kind of breakup. That's why she's so…"

"Combative?" Redinger supplied. "Irritable?"

He'd been about to say "fragile." Or had he been imagining that? It was possible that beneath her armor there was more armor. Still, he couldn't forget the tears he'd pretended not to see. Nor could he forget the smile that had lit up her face when she'd first proposed her deal. This was important to her for a variety of reasons. "On top of her personal troubles, Miss Wright's in financial difficulty. She's likely counting on the income from selling this story."

"I appreciate your concern, Sergeant Matheson. To be fair, we'll find a way to compensate her for her time. Is there anything else?"

He could see by the major's demeanor that he considered the decision made, which meant there was no room for discussion.

Tyler didn't understand why he was tempted to continue

protesting. Why would he risk questioning his commanding officer's orders on behalf of a woman he barely knew?

Why? Because strangers or not, he did know one very important fact about Emily Wright: She had a problem with trust when it came to men.

Damn. He wouldn't want to be anywhere near her when she discovered the truth about this deal.

Emily flung open the curtains, put one knee on the window seat and filled her lungs with the morning air. There were no squawking chickens or barking dogs to disturb the peace here. The small courtyard at the center of the private wing of the palace was as quiet as a painting. It even looked like one, with the traces of mist floating in the shadows beneath the orange trees and clinging to the cobblestones around the tinkling fountain. The flower beds were loaded with furled blooms awaiting the touch of the sun. The air held the humid bite of ozone. It would likely get as hot as the day before outside, but some clever pre-air-conditioning architect had put the bedrooms on the north side. The thick walls were cool to the touch.

Yawning widely, she twisted to regard the room she'd been given. Though it would be small by royal standards, it was more than adequate by hers. She chuckled. Adequate? That was an understatement. Lengths of romantic, rose-colored tulle swooped from a ring in the ceiling to frame the bed. Instead of a closet, there was a huge, hinged wardrobe that was carved from what appeared to be walnut and smelled of oranges. The tile floor, which had been sensuously cool beneath her bare feet, extended into the bathroom where there was a claw-foot tub that was almost as long as the bed. And there were vases of flowers everywhere, filling the air with exotic scents and flashes of color.

Oh, yeah, she could get used to living in a palace. She wasn't going to miss the Royal Rocaman Hotel at all.

She'd been delighted to see that Major Redinger had kept his word about the repairs. The lock on her hotel room door had been fixed, the bullet holes in the wall had been patched and the balcony doors had been replaced by the time she'd gone back for her suitcase yesterday evening. Everything else had been cleaned up and tidied, as if the attack had never happened. Amazing. Not only that, most of the deposit she'd shelled out for the honeymoon suite had been refunded to her credit card. She didn't know how the major had managed to get the hotel to agree to that. The travel agency had insisted that everything was nonrefundable. Obviously, the army had more clout than she did.

There was a tap on the door. "Miss Wright?"

Though he had spoken almost as softly as he'd knocked, Emily instantly recognized Tyler's voice. She pushed away from the window, snatching her robe from the floor as she passed the bed. "Just a minute."

She fumbled to tie the belt. The robe was new, like most of the things in her suitcase. The silk was as slippery as water and only fell to mid-thigh, but it was better than nothing. Then again, Tyler had already seen her in nothing, hadn't he?

She scowled, annoyed that she was still dwelling on that. She shouldn't think of him as a man. She had to think of him as a source. From now on, their relationship was strictly business. This story could change her life. Besides the possible benefits to her bank account and to her future career, the work was giving her something positive to focus on. And God knows, she needed that. This was the first morning in weeks that she'd actually looked forward to getting out of bed.

She yanked the door open. "What's going on?"

Tyler didn't answer right away. Instead, he gave her a long perusal from her bed-head hair to her bare feet.

Emily couldn't seem to find her voice, either. He was wearing a suit today. A dark gray one, along with a white shirt and a steel-blue tie that made his eyes look fabulous. His body was totally covered. Not so much as a hint of bare muscle or hair-fuzzed skin was showing, yet she knew it was there. She'd thought he looked sexy in a golf shirt and jeans. That was nothing compared to the effect of this large hunk of masculinity that was standing in front of her in a tailored suit and... She glanced down. He was wearing his cowboy boots. They'd been buffed for the occasion, but they still carried the scars of hard and probably interesting use.

There was something intriguing about a man who wore boots with a suit. As if he set limits on how civilized he was willing to be.

"My shift starts in forty minutes," he said.

She blew out her breath, then raked her hair off her face, curled her fingers and gave her scalp a brisk scrape with her nails. She needed to get some blood flowing to her brain. Strictly business, she reminded herself. The major had agreed to let her accompany the men. Obviously, he was being true to his word on this, too, so she didn't want to squander her first opportunity to get some good material. "What will you be doing?"

"Accompanying the envoy. She has a breakfast meeting with President Gorrell in an hour."

Norberto Gorrell, the President of Rocama. A genuine head of state. Emily needed a moment for the reality of that to sink in. No wonder Tyler was wearing a suit. "Where?"

"Here in the palace."

She fiddled with her belt while she mentally cataloged everything in her suitcase. God, what was she going to wear? Men had it lucky. All they needed was one suit and they were done.

"We'll clear the room beforehand, so we won't actually be attending the meeting," he said. "We'll be taking up a post in the hall."

"Okay. Sounds easy enough."

"We can't relax for an instant, Miss Wright."

"You don't think El Gato could get into this palace, do you?"

"We have to operate on the assumption that no location is completely secure."

She nodded. These were good quotes for her article. She should be taping them, but she hadn't brought her recorder. She hadn't brought her laptop, either. Not for a vacation. At least she did have her digital camera. She wished she'd thought to grab some of the hotel's stationery before she'd checked out. "Would you have a pad of paper I could borrow?"

"Why?"

"It's for taking notes."

He hesitated. For a moment he seemed uncomfortable. "I'll see what I can do."

"Thanks."

"Have you eaten?"

"How could I?" She waved her arm behind her, then grabbed the collar of her robe as it slid off her shoulder. "There's no phone in my room, not that I would expect the palace to have room service, but I'm pretty isolated here. My cell phone doesn't work, either. That reminds me, what kind of phone service does your major have? I noticed his phone worked."

"It's military issue. You can share breakfast with us. We eat in our quarters."

"I never thought to ask. Where are you staying?"

"Upstairs." He used his index finger to slide her robe back onto her shoulder. "First you might want to put on something that doesn't play peekaboo."

She shuddered. The silk had a mind of its own and wasn't that easy to hang on to, so he probably hadn't meant to trail the backs of his knuckles over her skin. "I'll try to find a dress without bullet holes."

He dropped his hand. "If you'd rather join us later…"

"Not on your life. A deal's a deal. I plan to take advantage of every minute."

The minutes seemed like hours. The first day of Emily's embedding with Eagle Squadron dragged into the second. Little changed other than the hall they were positioned in. She chaffed at the lack of activity, but it didn't appear to bother Tyler. When he was on duty he appeared as calm as a living statue. About as talkative, too. Currently, they were outside the conference room while the envoy attended yet another meeting. This one included a group of sober-faced men and women who made up the president's cabinet. The carved wood doors were too thick for the sound of voices to penetrate, so Emily couldn't guess at the topic.

Whatever it was, both President Gorrell and Helen Haggerty appeared to be deep in discussion, their gray heads angled toward each other, whenever they were together. Neither spared her more than a glance when they passed by, so Emily had stopped fretting about what to wear a day ago. She redid her ponytail, tugged at the cuffs of the cardigan she was using to make her sundress more respectable and looked around.

Vic Gonzales was teamed up with Tyler today. He stood

at the bend in the corridor, and though he seemed relaxed at first glance, he'd been as alert as Tyler whenever there had been a sign of movement. He had an expressive mouth and sparkling dark eyes that made him appear to be on the verge of a smile—he'd have to be good-humored to accept the nickname "Gonzo"—yet he'd been as reserved around Emily as the rest of the men. They had the neutral, don't-give-away-anything expressions of on-duty cops or football players on a Sunday in December. They were wearing their game faces.

The only exception had been the bald man who had been in charge of the monitoring equipment upstairs, Chief Esposito. He reminded her of her uncle Wade, not chatty but approachable. He'd inputted her description of El Gato into a computer program that he'd said he'd obtained from Homeland Security. Emily realized that by sharing her knowledge so early she had weakened her bargaining position. She hadn't really considered withholding it, though. She wasn't going to play games with an innocent woman's life. Thanks to the help of Duncan Colbert, who had some kind of connection with Army Intelligence, they'd managed to construct a good likeness of the assassin. It had been printed out and distributed to the entire team as well as to President Gorrell's elite palace guards.

Those guards were as no-nonsense as the American soldiers. Rather than suits, they wore tan uniforms that were belted at the waist with dark leather. They appeared to do regular patrols throughout the palace, as she'd noticed the same pair of men walk past the conference room three times this afternoon. And she was certain it was the same men, since she'd made sure to scrutinize them each time.

Tyler nodded and mumbled something she couldn't catch. A glance at Sergeant Gonzales made her realize they were talking over their radios again. She sighed and leaned her back against the wall. Her shoulder brushed the frame of a painting, knocking it askew. She straightened it, moved a few more inches to her right and tried again. She wished she could pass the time by snapping a few pictures, but the president's guards had forbidden her to take photographs in the private wing of the palace. "Is it always this boring?"

"Boring is good," Tyler said. "When things get exciting there's usually a problem."

"It seems we were in a big rush to get here and all we end up doing is holding up the wallpaper."

"It's the army way."

"Huh. 'They also serve—'"

"'Who only stand and wait,'" he finished.

She blinked. A cowboy who knew his Milton? "Let me guess. Your sisters made you read poetry."

"Something like that."

"By the way, where's that big gun of yours today?"

"I left my rifle upstairs."

She leaned sideways to study him. There were no obvious bulges under his jacket. Nothing that couldn't be accounted for, anyway. "You've got to be carrying a weapon someplace."

"We always come prepared for the job."

"You don't want to get specific, do you?"

"It wouldn't be relevant to your story."

"How would you know? A lot of readers would like to learn—" *What you've got hidden under your clothes.* She tamped down the thought. "They'd like to know exactly what a soldier does on an undercover mission," she finished. "Major Redinger said you'd cooperate with me, remember?"

He grunted.

"And that reminds me, you haven't yet told me what

kind of soldiers you are. Only the major wears a uniform. Are you from the Special Forces?" When he didn't reply, she tried again. "You might as well tell me, because I'm going to keep asking until you do."

"Yes."

"Ah. Okay, that's what I thought. You're commandos, right?"

"We're just soldiers, ma'am."

She glanced at the closed doors again. "Come to think of it, I remember reading something about the envoy's father when he was in the Gulf. General Haggerty used to move around with a group of Special Forces guys for bodyguards. He didn't really need them. He just thought they looked cool in their black outfits. He was able to make a great entrance whenever he walked into a room surrounded by his personal ninjas. I think they were from Delta Force." She focused on Tyler again. "Like you, right?"

"I was in grammar school during the first Gulf War."

"You didn't answer my question."

"Didn't I?"

"*Are* you from Delta Force?"

He hesitated, as he frequently did before he replied. Clearly he was weighing everything he told her concerning the mission. "Only Hollywood uses that name. The men you've met belong to Eagle Squadron. We're from Operational Detachment Delta."

She pursed her lips in a silent whistle. The Hollywood name was fine with her. This was better than she could have hoped. How many reporters got the opportunity to be embedded with Delta Force commandos? They were notoriously secretive. This story would be hot. Almost as hot as these commandos.

But that particular fact definitely wasn't relevant to her story, she told herself. It made no difference if each of the men she had met happened to be incredibly handsome in their own, individual ways. Vic Gonzales had his brooding, Latin good looks. Jack Norton had a lean and hungry predator aura. Kurt Lang reminded her of Wolverine without the hardware and bad hair, and Duncan Colbert could have posed for a book cover as a buccaneer. Of course, none of them came close to Tyler with regards to sheer, physical magnetism.

Tyler was looking at her mouth, which made her realize her lips were still puckered. She pressed them flat and took out the spiral notebook she'd borrowed from Chief Esposito.

"I have a question you haven't answered yet," Tyler said. "Why did you call El Gato the milkman?"

"Oh, that. He looked a lot like Ralph, the man who drove the milk truck to my parents' farm."

"Where's their farm?"

"Near Packenham Junction." She held up her palm. "And before you start with the jokes, yes, it's a hick town in Wisconsin whose main industry is cheese."

"Why would I joke about that?"

"Everyone else does. The name is corny enough to belong in a 1960s sitcom."

He shook his head. "Not if you come from Miller's Hole."

"Miller's…?"

"Hole. Wyoming. Named after Cyrus Miller's watering hole."

"Wyoming? Then I guess you came by that cowboy boot habit of yours honestly."

He gave her a sideways glance. "Occupational hazard."

"Touché."

"My family runs beef cattle, not dairy," he continued. "But the town's probably a lot like Packenham Junction."

"Back home, no one locks their doors."

"Sounds familiar. And does everyone know everyone else's business?"

"You bet. Who needs text-messaging when there's Dimitri's Pizzeria?"

"The main hangout in Miller's Hole is just called The Hole."

"Is it as bad as it sounds?"

"Good enough for us cowboys."

She smiled. "Packenham only has two gas stations."

"We've got three, but they take turns closing on weekends."

"Our cops take Mondays off."

"Our sheriff runs the bowling alley and video store."

"And every kid's ambition is to live somewhere else when they grow up," she finished.

He nodded. "That sums it up."

"Is that why you joined the army? Because you wanted to leave Miller's Hole?"

"Essentially. Is that why you wore the scuzzball's ring? To leave Packenham Junction?"

Emily's first impulse was to deny it, but then she forced herself to consider the idea. Christopher had been raised in New York City, which had been one reason she'd found him so attractive. He'd been different from the men she'd known all her life. He'd seemed more polished and worldly. She'd liked the fact that he hadn't gone to the same schools that she had. That had meant he wouldn't be familiar with the child she'd once been and so he wouldn't have had any preconceived expectations of who she should be now. He hadn't had a web of relatives nearby waiting to see him fail, either.

Oh, she knew her family meant well. They wanted her to be happy. They thought they knew what was best for her, yet how could they when all they focused on were her faults? They hadn't realized they were humiliating her by trying to match her up with someone's neighbor's cousin at every family gathering. They wouldn't understand that the more they told her something wouldn't work, the more she felt driven to prove them wrong. She was certain all the "I told you sos" that were waiting for her back in Packenham Junction would be said in the spirit of constructive advice.

Tyler was right. She'd been eager to shake off the ties of her hometown and had believed she could do that with Christopher.

And now she was adrift. No new husband, no job and no money. That's what she got for believing in dreams and for trusting a man. For one crazy year she'd lowered her guard and had convinced herself she was in love. But as everyone back in Packenham Junction knew, tough, sharp-tongued Emily Wright would never have fitted into a fairy tale. Not as the heroine, anyway.

Tyler touched her arm. "Sorry. It's not my business."

She swallowed hard, trying to push down the lump in her throat. She wasn't going to wallow. She'd done enough of that already. She had to get on with her life. This was already the third day of the rest of it. Now that Tyler seemed willing to talk to her, she shouldn't waste this opportunity to get some background information for her story. She busied herself with turning to a fresh page in her notebook. "I thought I was the one asking the questions."

He withdrew his hand and did a slow scan of the empty corridor. "Go ahead."

"You were saying that you enlisted to get away from Miller's Hole. Tell me about it."

"I was training for the Olympics when a couple of army recruiters approached me," he replied.

She was impressed. He definitely looked as if he could be an athlete. "What sport?"

"Biathlon. Cross-country skiing combined with target shooting."

"That's a Nordic sport, isn't it?"

"My maternal grandfather was Swedish. He got me on skis before I was put on a horse."

"Were you any good at it?"

"Not good enough to medal. I was better with a rifle than I was with skis."

"Ah, and that's why the recruiters wanted you?"

"Apparently."

"Do you like being in the army?"

"It beats mucking out barns."

"What do you like the most about the missions you do?"

He hesitated. "The variety. The challenge. We never know where we'll go next."

"Don't you miss your family and the ranch?"

"I do miss my family, but my father and brothers-in-law manage the ranch fine without me."

"What about your mother and sisters? Don't they have a say in the ranch? Or are the men in your family the type who think that women can't manage anything more than a recipe book?"

He muffled a snort.

Emily regarded him more closely. "What's so funny?"

"My mother's the one who taught me how to shoot. And the only things my sisters *don't* read are recipe books."

They sounded like interesting people. Even without meeting them, she was sure she would like them. "Are all your sisters married?"

He nodded. His lips softened into one of his almost-smiles. "The youngest one just last year."

"What about you?" she asked. "Is there a special woman in your life? Haven't you ever wanted to settle down and—"

She never got the chance to finish her question. She wasn't sure why she'd started to ask it, because she'd already strayed a long way from her topic. Her words ended in a gasp as Tyler caught her by the elbows and half lifted, half dragged her to an alcove on the other side of the corridor from the conference room door. "Stay here," he ordered.

"Why? What's going on?"

He pressed her back to the wall and released her as quickly as he'd grabbed her. An instant later, he was gripping a heavy-looking black pistol that he'd taken from somewhere beneath his suit coat. "Gonzo?"

Sergeant Gonzales was hurrying toward them, a similar gun in his hand. The guards who had patrolled the corridor were approaching from the opposite direction. Gonzales spoke rapidly in Spanish to them as they moved to flank the door.

"The room is secure, Major," Tyler said.

"Gorrell's men are sending the canine teams over here to do another sweep," Gonzales said. "They also want to initiate an evacuation."

"Negative. That might be what El Gato wants," Tyler said. "It's in the other wing, and it sounds like a small charge. Let me see what I can do first."

Emily hugged her notebook to her chest as the men continued to speak over their radios. She could feel her heart pounding against the cardboard cover. "Did you say charge? Are you talking about a *bomb?*"

Tyler pointed at Gonzales, then cocked his thumb at

Emily. "Watch her, Gonzo. If I give the word to move out, make sure she goes."

"No problem."

"Wait! Sergeant Matheson, I demand to know what's going on."

He had already disappeared past the bend of the corridor by the time she finished her sentence. For a big man, he moved surprisingly fast. She looked at Gonzales. "All right, Sergeant. Either you tell me what's happening or I go find the major so he can remind you of our agreement. Is there a bomb?"

Although she'd expected a positive reply because of what she'd just heard, seeing Gonzales's matter-of-fact nod made it all horribly real. Oh, God. Why had she ever complained about being bored?

"We should be all right here," he said. "The explosive's in the reception hall, in the public wing of the palace. We're waiting for Matheson's assessment before we risk moving the envoy—" He paused as the guards spoke to him in Spanish again. "Or the president and his cabinet to another location," he finished.

"His assessment? You mean of the bomb? No, that's too dangerous. What does he think he's doing? How can you be so calm? We should all be getting out and leaving this to the bomb squad."

"Ma'am, Sergeant Matheson *is* the bomb squad."

Two more guards approached, only these ones were accompanied by leashed German shepherds. They walked between Emily and Gonzales, blocking his view of her for a crucial instant.

Emily didn't stop to think. Taking a deep breath, she ran after Tyler.

Chapter 4

The glazed tiles beneath his back were growing damp, making Tyler's shirt stick to the floor. The lights he'd positioned around the work area were only adding to the heat that had accumulated in the reception hall over the course of the day. He'd already discarded his jacket and rolled up his sleeves to get more comfortable. Still, he knew that most of his sweat wasn't because of the temperature.

No matter how routine demolitions had become for him, or how many times he'd been called on to neutralize an explosive device, he knew that accidents happened. As Eagle Squadron's ordnance specialist, he accepted the risk his position entailed. That didn't mean he was willing to share it. This was one job he preferred to do alone.

Tyler used his heel to slide himself closer to the cabinet, then twisted his neck so he could get a better view of the bomb that was taped to the underside of the middle shelf. "It's got two initiators," he said into his mic. "One's electric, probably activated by a cell phone signal. The other's a time-delay pencil, old-school but reliable. Each has its own firing train."

"Belt and suspenders man," Kurt remarked in Tyler's earphone.

"It fits with El Gato's profile," Duncan said. "He's a thorough planner."

Redinger's voice joined the others. "What about the explosive?"

Tyler used the tip of his knife to pry off a sample of the white compound, brought it to his nose and took a careful sniff. "C4."

"What's your take on it?"

"It's a relatively small charge. The material isn't shaped or tamped. The location away from the walls indicates it was intended for anti-personnel, not demolition, but it would probably blow out this room. Could collapse the second story, too, depending on how sound the old beams are. Are the envoy and the president still secure?"

Gonzales joined the conversation. "They haven't left the conference room."

He felt a spurt of anger at the sound of Gonzo's voice. "What about Miss Wright?" Tyler asked.

"I've still got her," Jack said. "We're in the interior courtyard."

He closed his eyes and breathed deeply a few times to calm his pulse. He knew he shouldn't blame Gonzales for losing Emily. Once she had bolted, Gonzo couldn't have left his assigned post to chase her. He'd made the correct decision. Her safety wasn't the mission priority, the envoy's was.

Yet according to Jack, Emily had been on her way here when he'd intercepted her. What the hell had she been thinking? Hadn't she realized the danger she was putting herself in?

And all for a story that would never be published.

It killed him to see how earnest Emily was about gathering her material. This wasn't simply a job for her. She had grasped onto her work like a lifeline. Every so often there was an edge of desperation to her questions, as if she were forcing herself to talk so that she didn't have to think. It was the same with her wisecracks. They were another strategy to avoid dealing with what was really bothering her. She was a woman who didn't like to admit weakness to anyone, especially to herself.

His initial assessment had been right: Emily was emotionally fragile. It had to be due to her breakup. She must have really loved the guy to have been hurt that badly. At least Tyler hadn't lied outright to her. That was the only way he could ease his conscience while still following the major's orders. But justified or not, whenever Tyler thought of the farce they were perpetrating, he felt like something he might scrape off his boot.

Damn, he couldn't go there. Not now. "Okay, I'd say the risk of the blast carrying that far is minimal. They should be safest where they are."

"Looks like the bomb could have been meant to force them outside," Duncan said. "A diversion, just as you thought. Good call, junior."

"I'll relay the information to President Gorrell," Redinger said. "Can you disable the device?"

Tyler hitched his shoulders partway into the cabinet and studied the pair of detonators that had been sunk into the wad of C4. "Yes, sir." He reached back for the tools that he'd aligned on the floor beside him and felt around until his fingers closed on the pliers. "It shouldn't be a problem."

"Good. Keep me posted."

"Will do."

The radio went silent, though Tyler knew the channel was still open. The men had suspended their usual chatter in order to allow him to concentrate. He closed the rubber-lined jaws of the pliers around the antenna, deciding to disrupt the electric firing train first. He disconnected the receiver from the battery and was easing the wire from the detonator when he heard a muted crack.

He swore under his breath and focused on the remaining initiator. The bomb wasn't as simple as he'd first assumed.

"Sergeant?" Redinger asked.

"The backup trigger activated," Tyler said. "I just heard the ampule break."

"Bummer," Kurt muttered.

Tyler set down the pliers, dried his forehead on his sleeve and retrieved his knife. The time for finesse had passed. One way or another, this was going to be over in a matter of seconds.

Emily sat on a wrought iron bench in the shadows of the courtyard, watching the fingers of light from the setting sun inch across the roof of the palace. Her notebook lay untouched on the seat beside her, but it wasn't the encroaching darkness that had stopped her from working. She hadn't written a word from the moment Jack had passed on the news that the bomb had been disarmed, which had been at least thirty minutes ago. She'd been trying to calm down ever since.

That bothered her. So had the depth of her concern when she'd realized that Tyler was in danger. They'd only spent two days together. Three, if she counted their stakeout at the café. She barely knew him. And this sort of task was part of his job. Jack had informed her that Tyler was the team's ordnance specialist and had been trained to handle any number of hazardous situations. Jack had even gone on to describe several.

She couldn't begin to imagine the concentration a person would need in order to deal with a live bomb. Tyler would have to have nerves of steel. No wonder he always seemed so steady. Staying in control would be vital to his survival. She'd already seen him in action when he'd tackled her amid a hail of bullets in her hotel room, so she knew he kept his cool under dangerous conditions.

But he was no automaton. She'd seen hints of softness, especially when he'd been talking about his family. He hadn't been able to conceal his sense of humor, either. Just before he'd run off, he'd been smiling—or almost smiling—about his little sister's wedding. Too bad he hadn't had a chance to answer the question about his love life.

She drew the elastic from her hair, slipped it over her wrist and gave her scalp a quick rub. How many times did she have to remind herself? She was physically attracted to Tyler. What woman alive wouldn't be? But her emotions couldn't be involved. They'd been wrung dry by her experience with Christopher.

She dropped her head into her hands. She no longer wanted a man. Any man. She knew better than that.

"Hey, junior," Jack said. "I thought you got lost."

"Had a few details to take care of. What's the latest?"

At the sound of Tyler's voice, Emily raised her head and shoved her hair out of her eyes. He was walking past the fountain toward the bench where she sat, and in spite of what she'd just told herself, she felt a tickling thrill as she watched him approach.

He was holding his jacket over his shoulder by two

fingers. His tie was gone, his shirt was unbuttoned to the center of his chest and his sleeves were rolled back, revealing tantalizing expanses of taut skin. The deepening shadows made him look larger somehow, accentuating his athletic body and the chiseled contours of his face. He'd looked sexy in his suit. He looked even better with the suit messed up, as if he were coming home to her at the end of a hard day.

Stop it, she told herself. The man had just finished disabling a bomb. Of course he'd look messed up. What was wrong with her?

"The envoy's back in her quarters," Jack said. He pushed away from the orange tree he'd been leaning against. "The major's running interference with the Rocamans."

"Why?"

"Some of Gorrell's cabinet kicked up a fuss during the lockdown. They wanted to evacuate. Guess they don't know you the way we do."

"They'll get over it."

"Dunk and Kurt are in the plaza, trying their luck at cat hunting."

"I don't think they'll find him."

"Yeah. El Gato would have disappeared when he didn't hear a bang."

"Sorry to disappoint him." Tyler finally looked at Emily. "I'll take over from here, Jack."

Tension tightened the lines beside his mouth, although the rest of his face gave nothing away. She had a crazy urge to pull him into her arms. Was none of the men willing to acknowledge what a heroic thing he'd just done? She waited until Jack turned to go, then wiped her palms on her dress and stood. "I'm glad everything went all right, Sergeant Matheson," she said.

"So am I, ma'am."

She lifted her hand toward him, meaning to push back a lock of hair that had fallen across his forehead, before she realized what she was doing. She picked up her notebook instead.

A muscle twitched in his cheek. "Chief Esposito wants to see you."

"What about?"

"He has some palace security tapes he'd like you to look through. They're in our briefing room." He put his hand under her elbow and guided her to a wooden door in the wall. "We can get there faster this way."

Though Tyler's touch was light, she could feel the same tension in his fingers that she'd seen around his mouth. "Don't you want to rest for a while?" she asked.

"Why?"

"Oh, I don't know. Maybe because you look as if you just ran a marathon in your suit?"

"I was only doing my job."

"Right. It's all in a day's work for you. Getting shot at and disarming bombs."

"I didn't get shot at today," he pointed out.

"This isn't funny."

"I'm glad you realize that. I hope that means the next time you're asked to stay put, you'll do it." He released her arm to open the door and silently gestured for her to precede him.

A flight of narrow stairs rose in front of them. Evidently, the renovations hadn't gotten this far. Unlike the wide, airy staircase she'd used to get to and from her room, this one was lit by only a few dim fixtures along the walls and barely had space for two people to pass. It had probably been designed for servants to go about their business invisibly, and hadn't seen much change since the palace had been built more than two centuries ago.

She placed her palm on the wooden rail that served as a banister and started climbing. "Listen, Sergeant Matheson, I realize you might be annoyed because I ran after you, but—"

"You placed yourself in danger."

"I was just following the story." The door swung shut, cutting off the last of the daylight. She blinked to help her eyes adjust and continued upward. "I thought I'd be able to do it better from where the action was."

"Is this story so important to you that it's worth risking your life?"

"Is your mission?"

"It's not the same. I know what I'm getting into. You don't."

"You're just worried that if I got blown up, I wouldn't be able to identify El Gato."

"I won't deny that you're useful to our mission," he said. "You know that yourself. But while you're with us, your safety is my responsibility."

"I'll sign a waiver, okay? It'll release you from any liability."

"There's more to it than that. Because of your actions, Sergeant Norton was pulled off his assigned patrol route."

"What do you want?" she asked. "Another apology? Fine." She rounded the corner of the landing for the second floor and increased her pace as she started up the next flight. "I'm sorry I interfered, but don't you think you're overreacting? I didn't need you or your friend or anyone else to babysit me. I didn't mean to go near the bomb. I'd only wanted to stay with you."

"I didn't want you with me. If something had gone wrong, you could have been hurt."

"And you would have been *killed*." She halted and

turned to face him. He stopped two steps below her, so for once she was looking down at him. Not that she could see much, since the nearest light was on the landing behind him. "You've got a lot of nerve scolding me about safety," she said. "Doesn't the army have robots or remote control gizmos that can go poke at bombs?"

"I was closer. It was the best course of action. Didn't Jack explain it to you?"

"He said the bomb was meant to be a diversion."

"That's right. El Gato was counting on us evacuating. Otherwise, he wouldn't have put the bomb where President Gorrell's men would be sure to find it."

"Sergeant Norton said it was under a shelf inside a cabinet. I wouldn't call that easy to spot."

"The public rooms are swept twice a day by dogs that are trained to sniff out explosives. That's a fact anyone who took one of the daily tours would know. Even if the bomb hadn't been found and it had gone off, it would have served the same purpose. We believe El Gato found another vantage point near the palace and was counting on forcing the envoy into the open."

"It seems like a pretty convoluted plan. Why wouldn't he try to plant a bomb where the envoy is staying?"

"The security measures in this wing of the palace are tighter." He blotted his forehead with his arm. "Much of the public areas are overseen by the local police."

"The police. That's why you don't trust them, right?"

He inhaled slowly. "Let's talk about this some other time."

She peered at him more closely. "What's wrong?"

"Nothing. We should get moving."

Instead of going upward, she descended a step, bringing her face level with his. "You're not as cool as you want people to think you are."

"It was at least a hundred degrees in that reception hall by the time I pulled out the last detonator."

"That's not what I meant, and you know it. Staying in control all the time and showing everyone how calm you are costs you, doesn't it?" She touched her fingertips to the side of his jaw. "You're in knots."

He caught her wrist. "Forget it."

"I could tell you were tense when I saw you. I hadn't meant to argue with you."

"You could argue about gravity."

"That's how I react to stress."

He rubbed the base of her thumb. "Don't be stressed. Not over your story. It sounds as if Jack kept you informed. You didn't miss anything."

"It wasn't my story I was concerned about. It was you."

"You shouldn't have been."

"Don't you think I know that? Believe me, I didn't want to worry. I didn't want to dread every second that passed because the next one might bring an explosion. I hate the fact that I care what happens to you."

He shifted his grip from her wrist to her hand. He threaded his fingers with hers. "You care what happens to me?"

"It was a momentary lapse. I'll get over it."

"Why?"

"Because we're using each other," she said. "We got that straight days ago. I know what I want from you, just as I know what you want from me. There's nothing personal between us. I've got enough problems. And all of them were caused by a man. I sure as hell don't need to complicate the mess by imprinting on the first guy who comes along and flexes his muscles at me."

He pulled her down to the same step he stood on, curled

their joined hands behind her waist and brought her hard against the front of his body.

The sudden move left her breathless. For a minute she couldn't do anything other than stand there and absorb the sensations. She'd felt his body against hers before, and that had been when she'd been naked. But even that couldn't compare to the connection she felt now.

Tyler was as solid as she remembered. As strong, too. He was supporting most of her weight and his balance never wavered. He dropped his jacket and shifted sideways, placing one foot on the step below as he leaned his shoulders against the wall. "You were saying?"

She moistened her lips. "I don't need a man. I don't need anyone."

"Want to know what I think?"

"No."

"You're not as tough as you want people to believe you are."

He'd thrown her own words back at her, but she couldn't form a reply. She could hardly breathe. The heat of his body, the familiar smell of his skin and the hush of the narrow stairwell were overwhelming her senses.

"That attitude of yours is just armor," he said. "And you fire off words to keep people at a safe distance."

"Works for me."

"How's it working now?" He moved their joined hands higher, arching her back so that her breasts pressed more firmly against his chest.

A fresh wave of pleasure washed over her. She couldn't suppress her shudder. The smart thing to do would be to pull away now before this embrace went any further. But how could she? If she was honest, she had to admit that this was what she'd wanted for the past three days.

Her notebook dropped from her hand and cartwheeled

down the steps with a rustle of paper. It didn't stop until it had slid to the center of the landing. Instead of going to retrieve it, she slipped her fingers through the opening in Tyler's shirt.

He drew in a ragged breath. "Say something, Emily."

"What?"

"Push me away. Argue."

She felt the thud of his heart against her palm. "Why?"

"Because you're right. I don't have as much control as I thought I did."

"So you want me to push you away?"

"You'd better. The way you're touching me, I don't think I can."

"Well, too bad. If I want to touch you, I will." She rubbed her fingertips over the thatch of hair in the center of his chest. "You owe me that much, considering what you put me through these past few hours. And do I need to point out that you started all this? And that you're the one holding me?"

"Emily—"

"I don't take orders very well, Sergeant." She clasped her hands behind his neck. "So if anyone around here's going to do some pushing away, it has to be you."

Even in the dimness, she could see the gleam of his smile. Without another word, he tilted his head and kissed her.

In some faraway recess of her mind, Emily knew this was crazy. There were a million excellent reasons why she shouldn't be kissing this man. But oh, he tasted so good. Better than champagne. Better than strawberries with chocolate. And probably just as bad for her.

He kissed her as if he'd known her all his life, as if he understood what she wanted and guessed what she needed.

He found the perfect angle so their noses didn't squish. Just the right pressure to hold the kiss while allowing her to explore the shape of his mouth. And within minutes, he discovered how to run his tongue over the bow of her upper lip in a way that made her knees go weak.

Emily fumbled open the rest of his buttons, yanked his shirt apart and slid her hand down his chest. Muscles contracted under her palm. She hummed in delight as she traced the washboard ripples that hardened his abdomen. His physique was even better than she'd imagined. And she had imagined it. A lot.

Tyler sank his hand into her hair and brought it to his face. His chest rose as he inhaled. "Soft," he whispered. "Just as I thought."

She wasn't sure whether he was talking about her hair or something else. It made no difference. She was listening to his tone more than his words. She rubbed her nose along the side of his neck until she found the hollow at the base of his throat. She closed her eyes, enjoying the sharp tang of his sweat, and the underlying musk that was unique to male skin. "Tyler?"

He curled his fingers around her nape to hold her head in place and closed his teeth around her earlobe. "Mmm?"

She gasped at the teasing bite. "Nothing. I just wanted to say your name."

"I like that." He sucked lightly. "Do you like this?"

"Mmm."

His lips skimmed the shell of her ear, so she was able to feel his smile. He parted the sides of her cardigan and ran his knuckles down the center of her sundress, trailing the tips of his fingers over the curve of her breast before he cupped it in his hand. "Fits perfectly," he murmured. "I figured this, too."

For one of the few times in her life, she was incapable

of further speech. She twisted more fully into his touch, then shuddered again as he explored her nipple through her clothes. His long, slender fingers were as gentle as she'd once thought, but there was an edge to his caress. An urgency in his body. As if he were fighting to regain his control....

Recklessness seized her. She didn't want him to regain control yet. She flattened one palm on the wall behind Tyler and straddled his bent leg.

The sound that rumbled through his chest was part laugh, part moan. He braced his back against the wall, pushed her skirt to her hips and helped her wriggle closer.

The intimate position drove away any remaining rational thought she might have had. Her breasts flattened against his bare chest while her thighs rubbed across the fabric of his pants. The heat between her legs suddenly became an ache. Sharp. Imperative. Wonderful.

Kissing him wasn't anywhere near enough.

She slipped her hand down his stomach and reached for his belt. She had just unfastened the buckle when she felt a sudden breeze puff over her legs. A second later, footsteps sounded at the bottom of the stairwell.

She froze.

Faint voices drifted upward. "I'm sure someone must have seen him."

"Yeah, they were too scared to talk. The Juarez family's got deep pockets."

"It's Lang and Colbert," Tyler whispered. "Damn." He gripped her by the waist and slid her off his leg.

Emily's knees had turned to jelly. She stumbled backward and caught the banister.

Tyler brushed her skirt down to cover her thighs and waited to ensure she had steadied, then did up his belt and snatched his jacket from where he'd dropped it. He squeezed past her to the step below. "Go upstairs," he whispered.

She strained to catch her breath. Before she could move, two large silhouettes came into view on the landing below them.

"Hold it, Dunk. What's that on the floor?"

The man in the front stopped, then leaned over to pick up her notebook. "Hey, isn't that…" His words trailed off as he looked up.

Tyler descended the stairs and held out his hand. "Thanks, Duncan. I was just coming to get that."

Duncan Colbert handed the notebook to Tyler, then looked straight past him to Emily.

"The lighting's bad," Tyler said. "Miss Wright stumbled."

"And you just happened to be close enough to catch her," Duncan said.

"Nah, he couldn't have been close," Kurt said. "Must have needed to run. Look how hard the boy's breathing."

Duncan flicked one side of Tyler's gaping shirt. "Maybe he ripped off his tie and lassoed her with it."

"Think it's time we gave junior that birds and bees talk, Dunk?"

"Did you find any trace of El Gato?" Tyler asked.

There was a brief silence before the men accepted the change of topic and resumed their earlier conversation.

Emily's brain finally began to function again. She was grateful for the shadows and she hoped they hid her blush. She forced a casual smile, forced an even more casual wave to the men, then turned and ascended the stairs in record time.

What on earth had she done? What was wrong with her? She should be thankful for the timely interruption.

Yes, she was exceedingly fortunate that she and Tyler had been stopped before they'd gone any further.

And once her body cooled and this ache in her heart went away, she hoped she would actually believe that.

Chapter 5

The house had been designed to blend into the surrounding landscape so effectively, it had taken a while for Emily to realize that she'd been looking at a man-made structure rather than a hill. Nature was doing its best to add to the camouflage. Broad-leafed vines with red flowers covered the walls and much of the steel roof. Thick hanks of moss dripped from the eaves. No glint of glass remained in the windows, only a deeper darkness. It was hard to tell how long the place had been abandoned. At the rate it was being consumed, it would soon disappear.

She clicked off a few frames, then lowered her camera and rubbed her arms, oddly chilled in spite of the sunlight that filtered through the trees. They were almost the entire breadth of the island from the safety of the Governor's Palace. The clusters of houses and red-earthed farms that surrounded the capital had grown sparser the farther they'd driven. Apart from this empty house, she hadn't seen any signs of habitation for hours. Human habitation, that is. The rain forest was teeming with other forms of life. Something that sounded like frogs were making a racket from deep within the brush. Birds screeched from trees that crowded right up to the edges of the road. She hoped there weren't any snakes.

"Keep to my left, Emily, out of my line of fire," Tyler said, moving past her along the path that curved around the house. "And stay with us." He'd spoken without looking at her, his attention completely on their surroundings, as it had been since their convoy had arrived.

Emily understood his concern. Helen Haggerty had decided on a private outing today, without President Gorrell or any of his representatives, so the palace guards hadn't accompanied them. Tyler and the other commandos had formed a loose diamond around the envoy as soon as she'd stepped out of her car. When she'd started walking, they'd maintained their positions about five yards in front, behind and to the sides. Major Redinger was here, too, walking within the protective diamond a pace in front of the envoy. All the men carried their weapons ready in their hands. Instead of the long rifles or the pistols Emily had previously seen, they had squat, no-nonsense machine guns.

There was no disguising their role today. No civilized suits for them, or waiting around in hallways, either. They wore flack vests with their T-shirts and jeans. Their body language radiated raw, male power. Alert. Intense. Tightly leashed. Every one of these soldiers looked as potentially dangerous as the jungle they watched.

Emily's pulse gave a little hop, a purely female response to being surrounded by so much ambient testosterone. She steadied her hands and took a few more shots of the commandos in their formation, then swung her camera back toward Tyler. Dapples of sunshine lit his broad shoulders.

He looked strong and competent, every inch the trained warrior, yet in her mind she was seeing the man who had kissed her.

It was hard to believe they were one and the same. How could the hands that gripped that deadly looking machine gun have handled her body so tenderly? How could his grimly set mouth have softened in a smile, or nibbled her ear? He was back in control today. Apart from a warmth in his gaze when their eyes had first met, and the extra squeeze he'd given her fingers as he'd helped her from the car, he had been behaving as if nothing had happened.

And she was happy to follow his lead. As she'd told him already, they knew what they wanted from each other. They couldn't let their relationship get personal. They both had bigger priorities.

"What do you think of this side of Rocama, Miss Wright?"

Emily wrapped her camera strap around her wrist and turned toward the envoy. It was unusual to be addressed directly. After days of holding up the wallpaper, she'd been getting accustomed to feeling invisible. "It's beautiful in a wild kind of sense," she responded. "And a long way from the palace."

"Yes, indeed. It's refreshing." Helen Haggerty hadn't worn one of her typical power suits today. In her cotton tunic, capri pants and comfortable-looking orthopaedic sandals, she looked more like someone's vacationing grandmother than a high-powered diplomat. "I apologize for not speaking with you sooner," she said, lowering her voice as she fell into step beside Emily. "I only just learned that you're not a part of Major Redinger's team."

Emily glanced at the major, who had moved a few paces to their right. "Technically, I suppose I am part of Eagle

Squadron, Ms. Haggerty," she said. "At least until the end of this mission."

"I understand you had a close encounter with my would-be assassin."

Any grandmotherly resemblance vanished. There was steel behind the mild voice, as well as courage. Emily took the opportunity to study the woman more closely. Helen appeared to be in her mid-sixties, and though she'd allowed her hair to remain a natural gray, her face projected a youthful vitality. Rimless bifocals perched midway down her nose. Behind their lenses, her eyes were sharp.

Emily realized she was being studied in return. "I wasn't at my best when it happened," she said. "Otherwise, I'm sure I would have been terrified."

"It's very brave of you to agree to identify him. I appreciate your willingness to help a total stranger."

The compliment made her uncomfortable. Her ability to recognize El Gato wasn't really needed on this field trip, since anyone who approached in this isolated spot would immediately be a suspect, regardless of what he looked like. "Did Major Redinger also tell you that I'm a reporter?"

"He did. He assured me that he explained to you the need for discretion during my visit. He guaranteed that you won't be revealing any information that would cause problems."

"Yes, the major and I have an agreement. I'll wait until the mission is over before I publish my article."

"I'm glad that you understand. We've worked very hard to get to this point with the Rocamans. I would hate to see our progress derailed because of a premature announcement."

Emily shortened her stride to better match the older woman's pace. "To be honest, I wouldn't know what to announce, Ms. Haggerty. I don't know whether you've noticed it, but these men aren't a very talkative bunch."

The envoy smiled. "Yes, I noticed. It's an affliction that's shared by many military men of my acquaintance."

"I read about your father. He was a hero in the first Gulf War."

"The general was a good leader, but he'd be the first to tell you that it was the men he commanded who were the real heroes."

Spoken like a true diplomat, Emily thought. "Had you ever considered following in his footsteps with a career in the military?"

"Never. I knew from my junior year in high school that I would follow a different path to serve my country. That was when I ran for class president and lost. The next year I managed the campaign of the candidate who won." She reached into her handbag and took out a folded cloth hat. She shook it out and placed it on her head so that the brim shaded her eyes. "That was when I learned that my talent lies behind the scenes."

"You and President Gorrell appear to have a good relationship."

"I'm fortunate to be able to consider him my friend. Since he came to office, Rocama has made great strides forward. The level of literacy in the population is rising, as is the life expectancy and the average wage. There is great potential in this island."

Emily searched her memory for facts about Rocama, but most of what she'd learned had come from tourist brochures. She hadn't yet had the opportunity to look for a library or an Internet café where she could do research, since she spent practically all of her waking hours with Tyler and the team. Even when they were off duty, they seemed to find some task for her to do, like refining the composite image of El Gato, or checking more surveillance footage. "I understand the restoration project in Rocama City is part of the government's campaign to boost the tourist industry."

"Yes. There is also a project in the works to deepen the harbor there in order to accommodate larger cruise ships."

"That sounds great. It is a beautiful place." She started as an animal hooted from somewhere in the trees. "I'm surprised more tour companies haven't discovered it before this."

"Before the recent airport expansion, the runways hadn't been long enough to handle regular commercial flights. In fact, seven years ago, the country only had one principal industry," the envoy said, coming to a halt as the path ended at the front entrance of the house. She swung her hand toward it. "And this was its headquarters."

Emily focused on the house. Now that she was closer, she could see that it wasn't as old as she'd first thought. The elaborate wood doors didn't appear weathered. Not all the windows were broken, either. "I don't understand. What was this place?"

"It was the processing lab and distribution center for the Juarez drug cartel."

She rubbed her arms. Was that why she'd felt a chill when she'd first seen it? "Juarez," she repeated. "That name is familiar."

"Arturo and Leonardo Juarez were ruthless thugs who acquired an obscene amount of wealth selling cocaine. For years they ran their empire from this compound. They considered themselves above the law, but then Leonardo made the mistake of hijacking a plane carrying American citizens."

Emily frowned. "I remember something about a hijacking

in this area several years ago, but I don't remember hearing that a drug cartel was involved."

The envoy peered at her from beneath the brim of her hat. "No, you wouldn't have. Major Redinger and his men were discreet then, too."

"I don't understand."

"This will have to be off the record."

"If you wish."

"Eagle Squadron were the ones who raided this house and destroyed the lab."

Emily turned to look at the major, but he had moved off to speak with Jack. She caught Tyler's gaze and scowled. His expression didn't change. He was far enough away to be out of earshot and likely wouldn't know what she was annoyed about.

But couldn't someone have told her that they'd been in Rocama before? And that they'd raided a drug cartel's headquarters? Didn't they consider that information something a reporter doing a story on this mission would want to know, whether it was off the record or not? It was a lot more relevant than the smattering of personal details she'd managed to extract from the men so far. It helped explain why the commandos of Eagle Squadron had been selected to guard the envoy in the first place.

"The Juarez property has remained unoccupied since it was confiscated by the Rocaman government," the envoy continued. "I'm hoping to convince the president to put it to better use."

Juarez. Now she remembered why the name was familiar. Kurt and Duncan had mentioned it when they'd returned to the palace the evening before, after they'd failed to find El Gato. She hadn't pursued it then. She'd been too preoccupied with getting away from Tyler. "Was everyone from the Juarez cartel arrested?" Emily asked.

"The brothers are still in prison. Unfortunately, their network was extensive. Even though the corrupt politicians who supported them are no longer in power, elements of their influence remain active."

Another piece of the puzzle shifted into place. "They're the ones who hired El Gato. They want to stop you from developing this property, don't they?"

"That's what I have been told."

"Why? Is it pride? Or do they think they'll be able to restart their drug business from here?"

"Their motives are complex. I suspect there is a good deal of pride behind their opposition, yet most is due to practicality. An American presence on this island would almost certainly ensure they would never regain the power they once had."

"A presence?" Emily repeated, glancing around. "What are you hoping to do with this place?"

"Our government has wanted to establish a military base in this region of the Caribbean for years. This is an ideal site."

A military base? Tyler hadn't mentioned anything about that, either, but surely he would have known. That had to be another reason the army had sent commandos to act as bodyguards: they had a direct stake in the success of the envoy's mission. A base would have a huge impact, not only strategically but economically and politically, as well. This story was even bigger than she'd imagined.

It was frustrating to be learning about it only now.

"Would you consider letting me interview you when your visit is over, Ms. Haggerty?"

"I would look forward to it, my dear. It's the least I could do to repay your help."

Tyler strode across the darkened courtyard, through the arched carriageway and headed for the gates. There were

no official event...
The envoy had be...
Juarez property and...
president was dining...
quiet enough that Tyle...
even before he rounded...

She was standing toe...
guards, her fists on her hip...
It was a pose he was getting...
cared to be. "I thought your jo...
said. "Not in."

"I am sorry, *señorita*."

"This is outrageous. Let me talk to your supervisor."

"He would say the same as I."

"What are you worried about?" She slipped the strap of her bag off her shoulder and held her arms out to her sides. "If you think I'm trying to make off with the royal silver, go ahead and frisk me. Search my purse."

"*Señorita,* I only follow orders."

"You know who I am. You walked by me three times yesterday when I was standing outside your president's conference room."

The guard looked past her, his shoulders lowering in relief as he spotted Tyler approaching. "*Por favor...*"

Tyler caught Emily's hands and tugged her a few steps away from the guard. "What are you doing?" he asked.

"I'm trying to leave, but this person won't open the gate."

"He's following the major's instructions. Why do you want to go out?"

"Why should it matter?"

"Because your safety is my responsibility. That's why I'm here. Redinger was notified that you were causing trouble."

o go outside. What's the problem
k soldier, right? Tell him to let me

ll me where you're going."

at's not the point. I'm a free citizen, am I not?"

He guided her another step back and put his head closer to hers. "Emily, have you forgotten you're a potential target? You can't go anywhere unprotected."

She tried to tug her hands free but he hung on. She sighed. "I'm only going to the library, Tyler."

"If you're looking for something to read, there's a library in the palace."

"It's not for entertainment. It's to do background research for my article. I also want to look at the back issues of the local papers to verify some information."

"Why the rush? The library is probably closed by now."

"No, it's open until nine tonight. I checked with one of the maids. She told me it's on the next street behind the Royal Rocaman Hotel. I know the way."

Tyler looked at the plaza beyond the gates. It wasn't busy, but it wasn't deserted, either. The sound of guitars came from the direction of the café where he and Emily had done their stakeout. A group of teenage boys, kicking a soccer ball between them, were making their way past the scaffolding in front of the courthouse. More people strolled through the pools of light cast by the streetlamps. There was plenty of activity to give them cover, yet not enough to hinder him from keeping track of it.

El Gato had no reason to expect that either Emily or the envoy would be leaving the palace grounds this evening. He already knew they were looking for him, so he'd probably be lying low until he could contrive another opportunity to strike. Although the palace guards were enforcing Redinger's instructions to the letter, the risk to Emily posed by an outing was minimal.

Tyler nodded to the guard. "It's all right," he said, placing his hand at the small of Emily's back. "Tell the major I'll be going with her."

She didn't speak again until they had left the gates behind. "Well, I'm glad to see that I'm allowed out. For a while there I got the impression I was some kind of prisoner."

"We want to protect you."

"Sometimes it seems more like supervision than protection." The soles of her sandals slapped hard against the cobblestones. As he'd observed on more than one occasion, she tended to increase her pace when she was annoyed. "I get the feeling you and the team don't fully trust me," she added.

"Why would you think that?"

"Gee, could it be because I've interviewed every one of you and the majority of what I've been given is fluff and busywork instead of facts?"

He couldn't dispute any of her accusations. That was exactly what had been happening.

"I talked to Helen Haggerty today," she continued. "In the space of ten minutes, she gave me more worthwhile material about this mission than I've been able to gather in the past four days. It made me realize I haven't really pushed as much as I could have. I've let you set the pace with our interviews, and that's what's got me ticked off the most." She stepped in front of him and poked her finger against his chest. "She said our government wants to build a military base in Rocama. Why didn't you tell me that?"

"We're here to protect the envoy. What she discusses with the Rocamans isn't relevant to our mission."

"I doubt that. And why didn't you tell me Eagle Squadron had been deployed here before?"

"That was seven years ago. It happened before I joined the team."

"That's no excuse. The other guys would have known about it. And don't you dare say no one told me either of those things because I didn't specifically ask."

"I've answered your questions as well as I could, but remember I've been on duty. So have the other men. It always has to come first."

"I realize that. I've seen how serious your job is. But maybe you could try to remember that I have a job I'm trying to do, too. Just because I carry a notebook instead of a gun doesn't mean my work isn't any less important to me. Yet you and the other men think it's just fine to give me nothing but little tidbits about your childhoods or what you like to eat for breakfast." She poked him harder. "I've been holding up my end of the deal. I have a right to expect the same from you."

Yes, she did, Tyler thought. Not for the first time, he cursed the major's orders. Yet since the envoy had already given Emily some of the facts, he couldn't be faulted for setting the record straight. He slipped his arm around her shoulders and started her moving forward once more. "This isn't the best place to have a discussion. We're too exposed. We're going to draw attention."

"There you go again. Trying to distract me."

"I'm trying to keep you safe."

"And I'm getting tired of being put off. I'd like some answers, Tyler." She lifted her shoulders as they walked, attempting to shrug off his arm.

In response, he firmed his grip. "The closer we are when we walk together, the less chance there is of anyone overhearing us."

"I hope this means you're actually going to give me something worth hearing."

He steered her past the last of the outdoor tables of the café, then started on a curving route that would take them around the outskirts of the plaza and keep them away from the streetlamps. "I'll tell you what I can."

"Great. Begin with Juarez."

"Leonardo Juarez hijacked a jet in order to bargain for the release of his brother, Arturo, who was already in an American prison. Eagle Squadron rescued the hostages and took Juarez into custody. But you won't find any accounts of the raid on the compound in the public record. If that's what you plan to look for at the library, you'll be out of luck."

"There must have been something. Bringing down the Juarez cartel would have been big news in a country where the drug trade was the primary industry."

"Yes, there would be articles about the arrests and drug seizures, but not about Eagle Squadron's role in them. The Rocaman government didn't want that made public for political reasons."

"At least that's a place to start."

"Keep in mind that the raid would have had little lasting effect without judicial follow-through. Norberto Gorrell was the one who did the bulk of the work to smash the cartel. He was a judge before he won the presidency."

"The follow-through couldn't have been complete if seven years later someone from the cartel has the means to hire an assassin."

"We suspect someone connected to the Juarez family contracted the hit, but we don't know for certain who it was."

"I've asked both you and Major Redinger why you don't trust the police. You've both avoided the question."

He thought before he replied. There would be no harm in being honest about this, too. It might keep Emily safer. "It's no secret that the previous administration was corrupt. A large portion of the police force was on the Juarez payroll as well. That's something you would find in the local papers, since many officers were prosecuted or dismissed."

"So you must suspect there are still some rotten apples."

"We have to assume there are."

"Of course. That's how El Gato would have been able to get the bomb into the reception hall. You told me the public areas were patrolled by police. They could have been bribed to look the other way."

"That's my guess."

"And that's why you didn't want me to call the police when El Gato broke into my hotel room. They wouldn't have done anything."

"Worse. They might have enabled him to eliminate another witness."

She turned her head to look at him as they walked. "You really did save my life."

He smiled. "My pleasure, ma'am."

She looked at his mouth. "If the Rocamans want to develop a tourist industry, they're going to have to clean up the police force."

He lifted his hand from her shoulder to stroke the ends of her ponytail. "That's the Rocaman government's concern, not ours. We're only here to guard the envoy."

She started at the contact. "What are you doing?"

"Playing with your hair."

"There's no one around now. You don't have to hang on to me any longer."

He dropped his arm and took her hand. "It doesn't hurt to maintain a cover," he said.

"What?"

"Look around us. Most of the people in the plaza are in groups or in couples. They're out for an evening stroll. We should try to blend in."

"We're not a couple."

"To anyone watching we are."

"You know what I mean. You and I are not a couple. Our relationship is strictly business. I thought I should make that plain."

In spite of her words, her fingers warmed within his. And despite his best intentions, he vividly remembered how good her fingers had felt when she'd slid them across his chest...and when she'd opened his belt. "You're saying this because of what happened yesterday."

"Forget it," she said.

"I shouldn't have kissed you."

"I agree. I shouldn't have kissed you, either, Tyler."

"It had been a long day. We were both on edge from adrenaline. Given the circumstances—"

"There are any number of excuses. It doesn't change the fact that it was a mistake. That's why we should forget it."

He knew she was right. The smart thing to do would be to agree with her and end this conversation. He'd intended to say much the same thing all day, but they'd never seemed to have enough privacy.

Yet there was something about the sound of distant music in the tropical night, and the feel of her hip grazing his as they walked, that made him hesitate. He might have to continue the charade as far as her story was concerned, but this was one aspect of their relationship he could be completely honest about. "It's not possible for me to forget that kiss, Emily. From now on, I'll be remembering it every time I climb a staircase."

"Okay, if you want to get literal about it, I won't be able to forget that kiss, either. It was just an expression. But I do think we should clear the air. I don't want you to get the wrong impression, regardless of how I, uh, behaved."

"Ah, you mean you don't want me to think that you're a passionate woman."

"That's a kind way to put it. We're practically strangers, and I was crawling all over you like a bad rash. That's not like me. I don't normally—"

"Make love in a dark stairwell?"

"To be blunt, no."

"Who chose your wardrobe?"

"What are you talking about?"

"The red lace garter belt and the scrap of a bra I saw on your hotel room floor. All the lingerie I saw in your suitcase. That silky thing you wore the other morning that didn't want to stay on your shoulders. They're the choices of a woman who enjoys her sexuality."

They had reached the grove of palm trees that was across from the hotel when she stopped dead and turned to face him. "Oh, my God. Is that why you kissed me? Because you saw those clothes and thought I was easy?"

He swallowed a laugh at the absurdity of her question. "There's nothing easy about you, Emily. That's another reason I wanted to kiss you."

"What the heck does that mean?"

"You're strong. I find that very attractive."

"Strong?" she repeated. "You're way off base there. If I were strong, I wouldn't have bought all those pathetic clothes that you saw. I wouldn't have paid to come to Rocama in the first place. I wouldn't have trusted the last man who kissed me."

Tyler caught her chin. *He* was the last man who had

kissed her. He was surprised how much that mattered to him. "Why would you say the clothes were pathetic?"

"Never mind."

"Do you want to know what I think?"

"No, especially if it's going to involve some metaphor about armor."

"You've probably convinced yourself that you bought all that sexy underwear because of the scuzzball, but the truth is, you bought it for yourself."

"Of course, I did. It wouldn't have fit him."

He tapped his finger to her lips. "No wisecracks, Emily. No arguing, either. I know he hurt you."

"Right, and I let him."

"That's the real source of all this anger I've been seeing, isn't it?" he asked, moving his finger to the frown line between her eyebrows. "You're blaming yourself, not him."

"Why not? It was my mistake. I should have noticed what he was sooner. I should have realized it was all an illusion. I should never have trusted—" Her voice broke. She blinked hard and fanned her hand in front of her eyes. "Now look what you've done. I told you I never cry."

He pulled her closer to the nearest palm tree and clasped his hands behind her waist. "How did that underwear make you feel, Emily?"

"I'm not going to discuss—"

"Did it make you feel strong? In control? Like a woman who wants to celebrate her body?"

"When I bought it, and when I packed it, yes. When I looked at it again once I got to the hotel…" She rubbed her eyes. "I can't believe I'm talking about this with you."

"Why not? I've seen you naked. No amount of sexy underwear could improve on that."

She placed her palms on his chest. "Tyler…"

"Did he ever see you in it?"

She fell silent, then slowly shook her head. "No. I bought it for our honeymoon."

Tyler settled her closer. "Then he was your fiancé."

"Yes."

"And the wedding?"

"I canceled it. He'd never intended to show up to it, anyway. He'd just been going through the motions to keep me happy. By the time I found that out, there was nothing I could do about the deposits for the hall or the photographer, but I figured, why waste a perfectly good honeymoon?"

He dried her cheek with his knuckles. "So you came to Rocama on your own."

"Spent my wedding night on my own, too. How pathetic is that? And drank all the complimentary champagne and ate all the goodies that came with the honeymoon suite, even though I knew I'd regret it in the morning. But I was feeling so sorry for myself and so damn mad at the world and men and all the stupid fairy tales I'd been idiotic enough to believe in when I'd been a kid that I couldn't think of anything else to do. Going on a honeymoon alone was a lot better than staying in Packenham Junction."

He stroked her jaw, picking up more tears on his fingertips. The flow was quiet but steady, as if she'd been saving them up. "I'm sorry, Emily."

"Don't be. All of it was my fault. I made my own choices. I trashed my life because I trusted a man. Huh, imagine that. Me, Emily Wright, who can chew guys up and spit them out if they get in my way. Anyone back home can tell you that. I've been using words to drive males away since my first article was published by my school newspaper in the ninth grade. I don't have a romantic bone in my entire beanpole of a body. But I swallowed Christopher's lies hook, line and sinker. I gave him everything. My love, my trust and every penny I had."

"He took money from you?"

"Yes, indeed. Most of it, I'd inherited from my great-aunt Beatrice. Maybe it wasn't much by city standards, but it would have bought a nice house where I come from. That's what I'd been saving it for. Until Christopher came along, anyway. He was a buyer for a big antique dealer, and he'd claimed he had the inside track on a collection of rare coins that would have made us a fortune. It was an investment in our future. Our life together. Why wouldn't I help him out?"

"What happened?"

"There were no coins. I was scammed, Tyler. He'd done it before. That's what the cops told me. He'd been preying on single women since he'd flunked out of college. It was his pattern to use what he got from one victim to finance his pursuit of the next one. I'd thought we'd been living off his money, but it had been from the last woman he'd scammed. He'd barely waited for my check to clear before he disappeared. I had filed a missing persons report. The fraud squad showed up instead. That, as they say, was my first clue."

Though she'd tried to be flip, she couldn't disguise the pain in her voice. He laid his palm against her cheek, helpless to do anything but listen. "Did they ever find him?"

"I heard he was arrested two days before I came to Rocama." She inhaled on a shaky laugh. "Sometimes I think it would have been better if I'd found him in bed with another woman. Then at least his betrayal would have been personal. I could have pretended there *had* been passion between us. I could have yelled and thrown things. That would have been a more satisfying ending to our engagement than finding a bunch of cops in suits searching our apartment."

"It might have been a scam for him, but it was real for you. There's nothing wrong with wanting to love someone, Emily. Cut yourself some slack."

"Oh, no. The warning signs had been there but I hadn't wanted to see them. I should have known it was too good to be true. I should have realized he didn't really want me—" She stopped and pressed her lips together, then shoved away from him and wiped her eyes. "No. I'll save the rest of this for his trial. I'm not going to shed another tear for that bastard. Because *that* would be truly pathetic."

"Emily…"

She turned away. Her back was stiff as she fought to regain control of herself. "I'm going to the library now, Tyler. I'm going to do some research."

He slipped his arm around her shoulders. "We can come back tomorrow. You don't need to work tonight."

"Wrong. I do need to work. This article is the first positive thing that's come into my life for a long, long time. Right now, it's all that's giving me a reason to keep going."

Tyler brushed a kiss over the side of her head. The scope of her fiancé's betrayal was far worse than he could have guessed. The trust she'd shown by opening up about it was humbling. He wanted to apologize. He wanted to hit something. Hell, he wanted to get Emily alone and make love to her until she forgot about the last man who had used her.

Only, that would be him, too.

Chapter 6

Emily carried her notes to the window seat, sat at one end and loosened the belt of her robe so she could draw up her legs. The palace was already stirring. Quiet voices rose from the courtyard below as a group of gardeners in green coveralls weeded their way across the flowerbeds. Down the hall, a door closed quietly from the direction of the envoy's suite. She guessed she'd have another thirty minutes at most before Tyler came to let her know the schedule for the day.

She wasn't sure how she'd face him. It had been hard enough having to act cool the morning after their kiss. What she'd done last evening had been even more intimate.

She'd confided in him. That was something she rarely did. Confessions were considered community property in her family, indeed in much of her town, so she'd learned early on to keep the things that hurt the worst to herself. Although the bare facts of her farce of an engagement had become public knowledge back home as soon as the fraud squad had shown up, she'd never shared her pain with anyone. No one would have expected her to, anyway. She'd spent too many years honing her defenses and her reputation. Not many people bothered to look further.

Yet with a few quiet words, Tyler had opened the floodgate. She'd been helpless to stop before she'd poured out the whole sordid story. She should be feeling horrible and awkward and prickly enough to screw a set of sharp spikes into her armor.

Only, she didn't feel bad. She felt good. Better than she had in days. Weeks. Tyler had told her she was a passionate woman. A strong woman. Then he had listened without judging and had dried her tears and held her hand as if he truly cared.

She ground the heels of her hands against her eyes. Her imagination was running away with her. Tyler's sisters had probably taught him how to be a good listener. He was a nice guy, that's all. And for all she knew, his sympathy could have been in the line of duty, so her emotional state wouldn't stop her from helping the team identify El Gato. He'd said as much before, when they'd been on that first stakeout. And only yesterday he'd reminded her that his duty always came first. She'd be a fool to read anything more into it.

Taking a deep breath, she picked up her notebook and opened it to a fresh page. Regardless of how…therapeutic her confession had felt, getting material for her article was her only goal. She'd made that clear last night. It's why she'd gotten up at sunrise, so she could go over what she had gathered and start fleshing out her notes. It was already day five of the mission. Only another four days and it would be over. She had to keep her priorities straight, the same way she was sure that Tyler was.

She leaned over to read the sheet that was on top of the stack of printouts beside her knee. The pile was smaller than she would have liked, since most of the newspapers in the library archives had been in Spanish. This item supported what Tyler had already told her about the widespread corruption among the local police. Though it appeared the worst offenders had been weeded out, she was grateful that Tyler had stopped her from contacting them. She jotted down the main points, cross-checked with other articles to ensure she had the dates and names correct, then worked her way through the rest of the pile.

She intended to hold Helen Haggerty to her word about an interview when the mission was over. She would probably need to hold off on revealing anything about the proposed base until the government was ready to make an official announcement, so maybe she could combine that with an in-depth piece on the envoy. Either way, she would still have the jump on any other reporters. Who knows, if Emily were lucky, Helen might feel grateful enough for her help on this mission to give her contacts in the government that could lead to other stories.

Yet that was for the future. She needed to establish her credentials first if she wanted to work in the big leagues. It was the article on Eagle Squadron that was going to open the doors for her. Being embedded for this mission was the chance of a lifetime. The personal details that she had gathered about the commandos so far wouldn't go to waste, either. Describing the personalities of the soldiers behind the mission would add a depth to her writing that no mere press release could duplicate.

She closed her notebook, picked up her camera and began to click through the photos she'd taken during the excursion to the Juarez compound. She'd been frustrated by the restrictions on photographing within the palace, but as it turned out, she couldn't have asked for better lighting or a more dramatic backdrop for the team than the lush tangle of Rocama's rain forest. Though her camera was only a low-end digital model, all she'd needed for her job at the *Packenham Observer,* some of these shots could pass for professional quality. They would be more than adequate to illustrate her article.

She'd caught the major's granite jaw perfectly, as well as the silver at his temples. As she'd suspected, he looked pure military even in civilian clothes. She'd snapped a picture of Kurt Lang sharing a quiet laugh with Gonzo while they went about the grim business of checking their weapons. Another of Duncan and Jack, looking rugged and protective as the petite, gray-haired Helen Haggerty walked past them. But the best photo was of Tyler. He was walking ahead of her, with his head partly turned so that his profile was backlit by a shaft of sunlight. The effect softened his features in a way that hinted at the sensitive man beneath the controlled facade.

It was amazing how deceptive appearances could be. At first glance, Tyler looked cool and distant. Christopher had been the opposite. He'd been convivial and charming. Handsome, too, with soulful brown eyes and a ready smile. He'd liked to talk even more than Emily did. They'd met at an estate auction near Madison when she'd been scouting around for an antique washstand to fill an empty corner in her apartment. One cup of coffee had led to another, and they'd ended up talking until dawn at an all-night diner.

She'd been flattered by his attention. Looking back on it, she could see that very first marathon conversation had given him the key that had allowed him to play her. Because only a very lonely woman would stay up all night to talk with a stranger. He'd picked up on other cues and exploited them, too: her impatience with the limitations of her small town. Her restlessness with her job. And most important of all, her yearning to be loved.

There's nothing wrong with wanting to love someone, Emily.

She touched her fingers to Tyler's image as she remembered his words. He'd made it sound simple. Before her experience with Christopher, she might have thought so. Not any longer. Too bad she hadn't met Tyler first.

Yet if it hadn't been for Christopher, she wouldn't have come to Rocama and met Tyler.

Christopher had never told her she was strong. She suspected he wouldn't have considered strength in a woman to be attractive. He'd liked treating her as if she were precious and delicate. That had been a novelty for Emily, and it had lulled her into dropping her guard. He'd treated her gently in the bedroom, too. The sex had been satisfying, not spectacular, but she'd never known spectacular so it hadn't mattered. She had planned on building a life with him. There were far more important aspects to a marriage than sex.

Sure. So she'd told herself. Nevertheless, she'd been hoping to heat things up with her groom. That's why she'd chosen to buy a suitcase full of sexy clothes for their honeymoon.

I've seen you naked. No amount of sexy underwear could improve on that.

Her lips curved. Tyler could say the most provocative things and make them sound like fact. Then again, if the kiss they'd shared was anything to go by, sex with him *would* be spectacular.

Yet how much of what she was feeling was only a rebound from Christopher? She had to be careful. Her emotions were still too raw for her to trust them. And she couldn't forget that her association with Tyler would end along with the mission. It was pointless to feel anything toward him.

Emily switched off her camera, turned her face toward the window and took a deep breath of the muggy air. The gardeners who had been weeding the flowerbeds had finished their task and were heading out of the courtyard. It must be later than she'd realized. She slid her feet to the floor, deciding she'd better put on some clothes before Tyler got here, when movement near the fountain caught her attention. One of the gardeners hadn't left with the others. He was leaning over the basin at the foot of the fountain, his arm dipped into the water to his elbow.

That was odd, she thought. He glanced around in a way that seemed almost furtive. Maybe he wasn't supposed to be muddying the fountain by washing his hands in it, but if he were washing, wouldn't he be putting both hands in the water?

The man straightened up quickly and looked toward the second-floor windows. Something metallic gleamed in his hand. And for a split second, Emily felt the impact of his dead black gaze.

"Oh, my God," she gasped, scrambling to her feet. She knew that face. She knew that expression, too. It was as flat and indifferent as a snake's.

There was no room for doubt. Instinct bypassed her conscious thought and she was across the room before she knew it. She yanked open the door and skidded barefoot into the hall.

Jack and Duncan were at the far end of the corridor, already in position outside the envoy's suite. They looked toward her, their mouths slightly open.

Belatedly she realized she hadn't fastened her robe. "El Gato," she yelled, clutching the edges together. "He's in the courtyard."

"Are you sure it's him?" Jack asked.

"Yes. One hundred percent positive."

Both men took guns from beneath their suit jackets, but only Duncan ran forward. He pointed at Emily. "Stay with Sergeant Norton," he ordered as he passed by.

"He's dressed like one of the gardeners," she called after him. "Dark green coveralls."

He repeated what she'd told him into his radio, bypassed the main staircase and went to the door that led to the servants' stairs.

Emily had fastened her belt and had taken an involuntary step after Duncan when she was stopped by Jack's voice. "Don't even think about it this time, ma'am. You know the drill. For all our sakes, you need to stay here."

She whirled. "Then you warn him. I saw El Gato take something from the fountain. It could have been a knife."

Jack relayed the information through his radio immediately. Before he had finished, Emily ran back into her room and across the floor to the window.

The courtyard was empty. There was no sign of El Gato or any of the gardeners. She pushed aside her notes, grabbed her camera and climbed to stand on the window seat. Bracing one hand on the window frame, she peered straight down so that she could see the base of the wall. No one was there, either.

The wooden door at the bottom of the servants' stairs slammed open. Duncan burst into the courtyard, his pistol gripped in both hands. Seconds later, a pair of Palace Guards came through the doors from the first-floor portrait gallery. Several more came through the arched carriageway that led to the gates. The calm of the morning was shattered by the tread of boots and the crackle of radios.

"Emily, get down from there!"

She turned her head and saw Tyler striding through the open door to her room. She returned her gaze to the window. "I can't see him. I don't know how he could have gotten away so fast."

"Now!" he said, clamping his hands on her hips. He lifted her off the window seat and swung her to the floor. "What the hell are you doing?"

"You've got no reason to yell at me! I stayed put this time, just like Duncan and Jack said. I wasn't—"

"You were standing in the window. You were making yourself a target."

"I was trying to get a picture of him. I wish I'd thought of doing that before I ran out to warn— Hey!"

He took her camera and lobbed it on the window seat, then pulled her farther into the room. "Your story's not worth your life."

"It wasn't for my story. Having a photo of El Gato would help your mission."

"Leave that to us."

"Why are you still shouting?"

"Your door was wide open. You had your back to it."

"Duncan had just gone down those stairs. No one could have gotten past him already."

"If El Gato got past palace security, he could be anywhere."

"Oh, there's no 'if' about it. I saw him. Right outside my window."

"Dammit, Emily. You've got to be more careful."

Her sharp retort died on her lips. The worry on his face was unmistakable. She understood how he felt; they'd been through this before. She put her palm on his cheek. "Tyler…"

He steadied her face between his hands and kissed her. It knocked her breathless. It wasn't anything like their first kiss. He wasn't concerned about finding the right angle or being gentle this time. Without any preliminaries, he gave her one bold thrust of his tongue, filling her mouth with his warmth and his taste.

Her pulse leaped in response. She parted her lips in an instinctive welcome, drew him in hard, then gave back as good as she got.

He groaned and lifted his head. "Dammit, Emily."

It was the same thing he'd said before the kiss, but his voice had become a hoarse whisper.

She ran her tongue along her upper lip. It felt numb and tingly at the same time. Absolutely wonderful.

He pressed his forehead to hers. "I'm sorry. This isn't why I came here."

"Then why did you?"

"I wanted to make sure you were safe. We're locking down the palace while we do a room-by-room search."

"And I suppose you thought it would be a good idea if you started by searching my throat?"

He exhaled on another curse. "Frankly, I wasn't thinking."

"That pesky adrenaline again?"

"Something like that. Did I hurt you?"

"If you had, you wouldn't need to ask. I'd have bitten you."

"I might have enjoyed that."

She thought about closing her mouth around his tongue, and feeling its firm length rasp between her teeth as he pushed in deeper... Her pulse went to a whole different level and she swayed.

He cupped her shoulders. "Are you sure you're okay?"

She locked her knees to keep herself steady. "Of course, I'm okay. I'm not some weak-kneed, hothouse flower who wilts from a little tongue. But I'd appreciate it if you try to stop this habit you have of grabbing me and flinging me around whenever you want to. This isn't the first time you've done that and it's getting irritating. Nobody flings me around. Haven't you noticed how tall I am?"

"Emily…"

"And you need to work on this take-charge attitude of yours. I realize it's probably part of the whole soldier mystique but it would help if you take a few seconds to explain things instead of issuing orders and rushing out like—"

He kissed her again. This time it was a mere brush of his mouth over hers before he released her and stepped back. "I'm on your side, Emily. You don't have to keep fighting me."

He was wrong. She *did* have to fight him. Otherwise, she was liable to lose herself in these feelings that were swirling around them. She raked her hair off her face, then grabbed for her collar as her robe slid off her shoulder.

Tyler's gaze followed her movement. His jaw twitched. He seemed about to say something else when footsteps sounded in the corridor. Several men in palace guard uniforms strode past her room. One paused in the doorway, spoke briefly to Tyler in Spanish, then returned the way he had come.

Tyler moved toward the door. "Promise me you won't leave this floor, Emily. Don't wander around. Don't go near the windows. If you need something, ask Jack or one of the palace guards."

"Tyler…"

"And if you want an explanation," he said, taking his gun from beneath his jacket, "I'm asking you to do those things because I can concentrate on my job better if I know you'll be safe."

Emily watched him go, then hugged her arms over her

chest. Her heart was pounding so hard she could hear it swish in her ears. "You be safe, too," she whispered.

It was pointless to feel anything for Tyler, she reminded herself. The attraction between them was probably just an illusion, or a product of their circumstances. She shouldn't trust her emotions any more than she should trust a man.

Because only a fool didn't learn from their mistakes.

They found the body at dusk. It had been wedged behind a stack of oil drums at the back of the garage that housed the official government vehicles. The middle-aged man had been hired on the landscaping crew two months earlier. Before that, he'd worked at a small florist shop until the owner's son-in-law had been given his job. He'd had no criminal record or known criminal associates. Like the young construction worker who had been killed the day the envoy had arrived, he simply appeared to have been in the wrong place at the wrong time. And like the other man, he'd been strangled and stripped. The big difference was that this time, the body had been found within the palace grounds.

Tyler stood at the entrance to the garage and watched the taillights of the unmarked van bearing the remains move toward the rear gates. President Gorrell wanted to keep the incident under wraps, at least until the envoy's visit was concluded. He understood the gravity of the situation. El Gato had gained entry to the palace *before* he'd disguised himself as a gardener. From what Emily had witnessed, he'd also had a weapon stashed in the fountain. The only way he could have accomplished either of those things was if he'd had inside help.

"The last team checked in." Esposito's voice came over the radio. "They drew a blank."

The chief had been overseeing the communications

during the search. He'd used the floor plans of the palace to chart the sweep pattern so that all the nooks and hidden corners were covered in order. Eagle Squadron had joined forces with every available member of the palace guards, moving methodically from east to west in a way that would prevent their quarry from doubling back to an area that had already been cleared.

Despite all the precautions, it appeared that El Gato had slipped out of their grasp again.

"I don't like the smell of this," Duncan said, falling in beside Tyler as he left the garage.

"I know what you mean. We need to take a closer look at the palace staff."

"I'm already on it. I've got Intelligence running another check on everyone who does business here. They've got to dig deeper."

"He must have used a vehicle to get past security. Besides the grounds and household employees, there would be delivery and maintenance trucks."

"And limos. We can't forget the politicians. Not everyone in the government supports Gorrell's policies. That's the problem with a democracy."

Tyler considered that for a while. "You might be on the right track. If the Juarez cartel wants to make a comeback, they'd need at least one friend in the legislature."

"It's no wonder Gorrell wants our help. This could be why we always seem to be one step behind El Gato. We still don't know what he'd been intending once he got inside today. That bothers me."

"The sniffer dogs went over every inch that the search teams did, so we know he didn't plant another explosive device. I'd bet he planned a direct attack."

"If we hadn't thrown off his game with our search, there

could have been a few more stripped bodies as he worked his way closer to the envoy."

Tyler scanned the windows of the palace as they approached. The ones on the ground floor were locked up tight, but many of the upper story ones were open to the night breeze. "He might still be here."

"Possible, but not probable. Even if he is, he won't be able to get to the envoy's quarters. Gonzo said the major put that entire corridor off-limits to the palace staff for the remainder of her visit."

"Then Emily should be safe, too."

"It's incredible that she spotted him in the first place. What were the odds she'd be up at dawn and happened to be looking out her window at the exact time he was in sight?"

Tyler rubbed his face, trying to drive out the image of Emily standing on the window seat with her camera. She truly hadn't considered the possibility that she could have been placing herself in danger. "We got lucky. It was a close call."

"Closer than you realize. I hadn't believed her at first. I thought it would turn out to be a false alarm."

"Emily isn't the type who would cry wolf. She wouldn't have said anything if she hadn't been certain."

"Well, she was right this time. That calling card El Gato left in the garage is proof enough."

"She's a courageous woman."

"Uh-huh. She's got great legs, too."

Tyler tightened his jaw. Emily did have exceptionally long, shapely legs. That short robe she'd been wearing this morning had displayed them to perfection. That was another reason the image of Emily on the window seat had been haunting him.

"She has interesting taste in underwear," Duncan

continued. "Take that red lace number I saw under her robe—"

"You shouldn't have noticed," Tyler cut in.

"It was about as subtle as a fire engine. That made it tough to miss."

He gave Duncan a stony look. "Try harder."

Duncan returned his regard without flinching. "You should take your own advice, junior. Seems to me you've been doing a lot more than noticing."

Tyler remained silent.

"Whatever's going on with you two," Duncan said, "don't forget why she's here."

He couldn't take offense at the reminder. The other men had a right to expect him to direct all of his attention to the mission. He'd given similar advice to Jack last fall, when his friend had grown too close to the woman who'd been in his charge. Jack had ignored the warning. Tyler couldn't. "No chance of that, Dunk. I know exactly why she's here, even if she doesn't."

By the time they reached their top-floor field headquarters, the major had returned, as well. Along with Esposito, he was studying the blueprints that someone had tacked to the walls of their briefing room over the course of the day. While Duncan helped himself to coffee and took a seat in front of his computer, Tyler went straight to Redinger. "Major?"

He rolled his neck wearily as he turned. "What is it, Sergeant?"

"If you have a minute, sir, I'd like to talk to you about Miss Wright."

"She did well today."

"That's for sure," Esposito interjected, crossing his arms as he leaned one shoulder against the wall. "Not many civilians would have been able to make that identification and then to act on it so quickly."

"Miss Wright's only thought was to help us," Tyler said. "Because of her, we probably derailed another assassination attempt."

"That's a given," the major said. "Ms. Haggerty has already expressed her gratitude. What's on your mind, Matheson? It's been a long day."

"Miss Wright deserves more than our thanks." He paused. "She also deserves our honesty."

Redinger used his foot to hook one of the stools that were in front of the communications equipment and dragged it closer, then sat. "You're referring to the problem of her newspaper article."

"Yes, sir. She has proven how cooperative she is, and I'm sure she can be trusted to act responsibly. The behavior we saw when she first joined us was only a reaction to a personal problem she's trying to work through."

"I recall you suspected some kind of breakup."

"It was more complicated than that. Before she came to Rocama, she was swindled out of her life savings by a man she'd been engaged to."

Duncan set his coffee down and swiveled his chair to face them. "Well, that explains her attitude toward men."

"And her short temper," Esposito added. He folded the wrapper over the chocolate bar he was eating and put it in his pocket. "The poor kid. Did they ever catch him?"

"He's awaiting trial."

"Bummer," Kurt said, moving into the room. "No wonder she needed a vacation."

Tyler glanced behind him to see that Jack had also returned and was listening. He'd only intended to talk to the major, yet it was just as well the other men heard the facts, too. All of them were involved in the charade. They should understand the toll it was going to take. "Her fiancé betrayed her trust on every level, which is why she was so cautious about us. The longer we lie to her about her story, the worse it's going to be for her when she learns that we're scamming her, too."

Duncan whistled through his teeth. "Whoever tells her had better put on a flack vest first."

"That's probably going to be you, junior," Jack said.

"I'm not worried about what she'll do to me, I'm worried about what this will do to her. The person she'll be the hardest on is herself."

"It may be difficult for her to accept initially," Redinger said. "But what's important is she'll be alive. With her continued cooperation, Ms. Haggerty will be, too. That's our priority. In time, Miss Wright should be able to understand we acted in her best interests."

"Does the end justify the means?" Tyler asked.

Redinger stood. His voice chilled. "Careful, Matheson."

"I mean no disrespect, Major. I just want to be fair to Miss Wright."

"Then use your head. We can't risk the success of the mission by alienating our only witness, particularly after she has just demonstrated how valuable she is. We need to bring her further in, not drive her out. In addition, her actions today have made her an even bigger target for El Gato. He doesn't leave loose ends. How long do you think she'll last on her own if you tell her the truth now and she decides to walk?"

Tyler couldn't give him an answer, because there *was* no right answer.

"We carry on as we started," Redinger said.

"Yes, sir."

"Unless you are requesting to be relieved of your duty."

"No, Major Redinger. Miss Wright is my responsibility. I would like to see this through to the end."

Chapter 7

"My dear, you look stunning."

Emily fidgeted with the fine chain that made up the strap of her gold evening bag. The petite envoy was the epitome of elegance in her royal blue taffeta gown. The discreet rustling of the fabric as she walked made her sound as classy as she looked. Next to her, Emily suspected she resembled an Amazon. "Thank you, Ms. Haggerty. That's kind of you to say."

"Nonsense, I'm not being kind, I'm being factual." The envoy tilted her head to smile up at her. "Only a woman with your height and coloring could wear a dress like that."

Emily hooked the chain on her shoulder and resisted the urge to fidget with her dress, too. The outfit had been a splurge for her, one she'd planned to wear for a romantic dinner with Christopher during their honeymoon. She hadn't cared that the slinky jade fabric would cost a fortune to dry-clean, or that the lack of sleeves and the scooped back displayed an acre of freckles. She hadn't hesitated to buy new shoes to go with it, either, even though she didn't normally wear heels this high, and the dainty gold straps that circled her ankles and toes were beginning to feel like iron bands. Like the other clothes she'd packed, she'd indulged herself because she'd wanted to spark a fire in her groom.

And of course, the main reason she'd chosen this outfit was because she'd loved the way it made her feel.

Like a woman who wants to celebrate her body.

Her lips quirked as she remembered Tyler's comment about her underwear. Though she wouldn't have put it quite that way, it was true. This dress did make the most of the attributes she had. As long as she didn't break her ankle by falling off these heels, that is.

"All clear." Tyler's voice came from behind her right shoulder. "We're proceeding to the ballroom now."

Emily's smile dimmed. The commandos had formed into a diamond around her and the envoy as soon as they'd moved from the private wing of the palace to the public one. The need for the extra security measures was a sobering reminder that El Gato had already managed to breach palace security twice.

She might have bought her glam jade-and-gold outfit with the hopes of kick-starting a little romance, but tonight had to be all business. The party they were attending with the envoy was black tie. That was the only reason Emily was wearing these clothes. Same with Tyler. Like the major, he hadn't put on a tux because he wanted to look good. He was wearing it because he needed to blend in with the other guests.

But oh, he did look good. Six feet four inches of black-clad, broad-shouldered, narrow-hipped masculine perfection. The major was almost as impressive. The rest of the team wore the same white jackets and black pants as the catering staff on the theory that waiters weren't normally noticed. Emily thought it was a wasted effort. If any of the men of Eagle Squadron sincerely thought they would blend into the crowd, then they must have assumed that any women who were attending were going to be blindfolded.

"Ms. Haggerty," Major Redinger said, halting at the ballroom doors. "We will try to remain unobtrusive, but remember that I or one of my men will be within a few steps of your side throughout the evening."

The envoy patted his sleeve. "Thank you for your concern, Major, but I have business to conduct. Please, try not to stay too close or you'll cramp my style."

Redinger signaled to the guards who were positioned outside the grand ballroom. Minutes later, he was escorting Helen Haggerty through the glittering crowd to be greeted by President Gorrell and his wife.

Although Emily had been living in the luxury of the palace for over a week, the scene she looked on now was beyond anything she'd experienced so far. She took a few moments to let it soak in. The room itself was spectacular, from its polished black marble floor to the crystal chandeliers that hung from the vaulted ceiling. Mirrors along the walls reflected the plaster columns and multiplied the size of the crowd. From a gallery at the far end, a group of musicians filled the air with classical music that blended tastefully with the hum of conversation.

She'd been told the guests would include politicians, diplomats and the cream of Rocaman society. That was easy to believe, considering how richly everyone was dressed and how decorously they were behaving. And though she'd seen President Gorrell numerous times as he'd passed her in the halls, she'd never seen him look so dignified or, well, presidential. A sash of office lent a regal air to his tuxedo. He stood out, even amid the cluster of distinguished-looking men and women who were vying for his attention.

"Emily," Tyler said. "We need to do a circuit of the room. We'll begin on the left."

She started forward. Except for Major Redinger, who had remained near the envoy, Emily was no longer able to see any of the other commandos. Apparently, she'd been wrong: it *was* possible to lose track of men who looked like that. "Where'd everyone go?"

"The rest of the team's in position."

"What does that mean?"

"We divided the room into quadrants before we got here. Each of the guys concentrates on one section."

"Ah, like the officiating crew on a football field. They each have their own area to keep track of."

"Exactly. On a security job like this, the men would either be moving through their sector or watching from a secure vantage point for anyone who looks or acts suspicious."

"Define suspicious. Besides pulling out a gun and opening fire."

"That would be a tip-off, all right. What we're watching for first is behavior. Body language. Patterns of movement. Anything that doesn't appear to belong."

"That makes sense. I noticed El Gato the other day mainly because his body language seemed furtive."

"We'll be starting with that, but we're also counting on your ability with faces. You're our ace in the hole. See that knot of people at the refreshment table?"

"Uh-huh."

Tyler settled his hand at the small of her back. "We're

going to circle around them to give you a chance to check everyone out."

Emily did her best to focus on each face as they passed, but she noticed nothing suspicious except the hair on a thin man beside the ice sculpture. He had one of the worst toupees she'd ever seen. "This may be a stupid question, but did anyone think to check under the table?"

"The dogs swept the room three times today. If anyone or anything was concealed, they would have sniffed it out."

"Okay."

"Relax," he said, moving his hand slightly higher. "I'm not going to let anything happen to you."

Though most of his hand still rested on her dress, his thumb brushed the bare skin of her back above the fabric. The contact gave her an unexpected jolt. Off balance, she teetered sideways.

Tyler grasped her hand and tucked it into the crook of his elbow, but not before his arm bumped the side of her breast. "Are you okay?"

She tried to ignore the spurt of pleasure from that contact, too. Not easily done, since she was also trying not to feel the tantalizing curve of the muscles beneath the sleeve where her fingers rested. "I'm fine. I just hadn't planned on doing a security patrol in these shoes when I bought them, so pardon me if I slow you down."

"Emily—"

"Then again, the extra height does help me see over the crowd, so maybe I should get the major to reimburse me for them, considering how they're going to be so helpful to your mission. He did spring for your tux rental, didn't he?"

"Whatever you paid for those shoes was worth it. Do you have any idea how sexy your legs look?"

He'd spoken quietly, his voice a low rumble beside her ear. She turned her head.

He wasn't looking at her. He was surveying the room as they walked, so she took a moment to enjoy his profile. This was another advantage to wearing heels. They gave her a better view of his face.

Oh, he looked more than merely good in that tux. He looked fabulous. The crisp white shirt made his skin glow and his eyes sparkle. His hair gleamed like gold as they passed beneath one of the chandeliers. In fact, against the backdrop of the ballroom, he was handsome enough to have stepped out of an illustration in a storybook....

Stop it, she told herself. Until a month ago she'd believed that Christopher was her Prince Charming, and look how that had turned out. "Thank you," she said. "You cleaned up pretty well yourself. But I don't understand how you keep getting away with wearing those cowboy boots. Don't you *ever* take them off? No, wait. You'd have to take them off when you ride into town for your Saturday night bath, right?"

The corner of his mouth curved in an almost-smile. It winked out a second later. "Ten o'clock. Short dark-haired man in a waiter's jacket. Tell me what you think."

Emily's stomach tightened at the change in Tyler's tone. She curled her fingers more firmly around his arm and moved her gaze to where he had indicated.

She spotted the man immediately. He was standing near the stairs that led to the musicians' gallery. She could see why Tyler had noticed him: he was the same height and had the same body type as El Gato. But one look at his wide-set eyes and the unscarred chin made her certain it wasn't him.

She blew out her breath. "No. El Gato's eyes are closer together."

He pressed her forearm against his side. "Don't get frustrated. It's seldom that easy."

"Maybe he's given up."

"Not if the Juarez family is paying his fee. They're not the kind of people even someone with El Gato's reputation would want to cross."

"But he couldn't possibly get in here. It's not as if this party is open to the public. Those guards at the doors aren't letting anyone in who doesn't belong. They even scrutinized us, for heaven's sake."

"That's their standard operating procedure at any event the president is attending."

"Which is the point I'm trying to make. Anyone would be nuts to think they could sneak past them."

"The envoy leaves Rocama tomorrow." He reversed direction as they neared the back of the hall and started on a route that would take them closer to the group around the envoy. "El Gato doesn't have many opportunities left if he's going to fulfill his contract. The major figures he'll have to make a move before the end of the night."

Which was the only reason she was here, in her drop-dead gorgeous gown, with her to-die-for escort. The reminder twisted another knot into her stomach. The days since she'd spotted El Gato in the courtyard had flown past. The mission was nearly over. So was her association with Tyler...whatever that was. Although the physical attraction between them showed no signs of dimming, there was also professional respect on both sides, as well as a deepening friendship. She liked him and was comfortable with him. She'd come to look forward to their daily sparring, and she was fairly certain that he did, too. Which was why she'd avoided thinking about the fact it was going to end.

Yet end it would. The envoy was scheduled to leave for Washington tomorrow evening. Once she was safely off

Rocaman soil, Eagle Squadron would pack up their gear, disassemble their field headquarters and return to their base in North Carolina tomorrow night. And the day after that, Emily would board her scheduled flight to Wisconsin. They would all go their separate ways. Get back to their separate lives.

She forced her thoughts back to business. "I've been wondering about the Juarez cartel's opposition to the proposed base," she said.

"What about it?"

"How could they believe they'd be able to stop it from being built by killing Helen Haggerty? Sure, she and President Gorrell have a good personal relationship, and I think she's a great lady so I hate to speculate what would happen if El Gato succeeded, but if he did, wouldn't our government send someone else to complete the negotiations she had started?"

"They would."

"Then why hire an assassin when the best they could hope for is a temporary delay?"

"That's a good question. It's possible they're underestimating American determination. Drug cartels have always used intimidation as a means to power."

"They use money, too," she said. "Before Gorrell was elected, cocaine production was Rocama's major industry. The profits bought a lot of police and politicians."

"Money's a big factor in another sense. The annual rent from a military base would provide a guaranteed source of funds for the government. So would the increased tourism. The more stable the country becomes, the more foreign investment they'll be able to attract."

Emily focused on the people around the envoy and the president as Tyler guided her nearer. "And as the wealth of the nation goes up, the less influence the Juarez people would be able to have," she said. "They might have realized the base could be a tipping point and they hired El Gato out of desperation."

"It does sound like a tactic of last resort. They would have to know that if they harm an American citizen, we'll hunt them down."

"The way Eagle Squadron captured Leonardo Juarez?"

"That's right. We don't follow the same rules that hamper law enforcement agencies. We do whatever's necessary for the success of our mission."

She smiled. "Thanks, Tyler."

"What for?"

She squeezed his arm. "For giving me straight answers. I'll probably end up quoting that last bit you said about doing whatever's necessary. I'm glad you're not weighing everything you tell me anymore. It really was annoying."

He halted and turned to face her. Instead of scanning the crowd, he kept his gaze steady on hers. His jaw twitched, as it often did when he was deciding what to say.

"It's okay," she said, giving him a smile. "I'm not trying to pick a fight this time, although I will if you're getting bored. It's been a while since our last one and I could probably use the practice."

He didn't return her smile. "I've always realized how important writing this article is to you, Emily, but we both have priorities that we need to put first. I hope you'll remember that when the mission is over."

It had sounded like an apology. She studied him, trying to read his expression, but his game face was firmly in place. "What's that supposed to mean?"

"Just what I said." He shifted his gaze past her shoulder.

"Tyler?"

"There's a short man walking toward the envoy. He's

carrying two champagne glasses. He's not dressed as a waiter."

Once again, Tyler's tone had hardened. Emily turned her head. She caught only a glimpse of the man who was approaching before a white-haired couple moved in her way. She stepped to the side but Tyler clamped his hand on her wrist to stop her.

"Stay with me," he said. "Tell me if you see him."

She stretched her neck just as the couple moved on. She tensed as the man walked into view. The height, weight, thick hair, even the walk were right for El Gato. She concentrated on his face and felt a stirring of recognition. Not alarm, though. "It's not him," she said. "But I've seen that man before."

"Where?"

As if he sensed their scrutiny, the man glanced their way. He smiled and changed course, walking directly toward them.

It took a moment for the memory to click. "Here in the palace," she said. "He was at the meeting in the conference room the day you disarmed the bomb. He must be a member of Gorrell's cabinet."

Tyler didn't relax. "Keep to my left," he told her. "I don't like the look of this guy."

To his left, she thought. That was so she wouldn't get in the way if he needed to draw his gun with his right hand. He'd explained that before. "I told you, he's not El Gato. He's just a politician."

The man reached them a moment later. He smiled widely, displaying a dazzling array of expertly capped teeth. "Good evening, *señorita*. I hope you are enjoying yourself?"

"Yes, thank you."

"Permit me to introduce myself." He bowed from the

waist, holding his arms out at his sides so he wouldn't tip the glasses he held. "I am Santiago Kenyon, the minister of culture. You are part of Ms. Haggerty's entourage, I believe? I noticed you arrived with her."

She wasn't sure how to reply. Tyler beat her to it. "Yes, we accompanied the envoy," he said.

Kenyon acknowledged Tyler with a nod while he kept his smile aimed at Emily. He appeared to be in his fifties, and had well-formed lips, a bold nose and thickly lashed dark eyes. He had the air of a man who considered himself to be irresistible.

Or maybe she got that impression because something about his eyes reminded her of Christopher. She unconsciously inched closer to Tyler's side.

"We have many art treasures in Rocama that date back to our colonial days," Kenyon said. "Have you had the opportunity to visit our national museum?"

"Not yet," she replied. "I'm afraid work must come first."

"Of course, of course. But certainly you could spare the time to view the pieces that are on display in the palace. There are many priceless works that adorn the walls. I am confident a woman of your beauty would appreciate our collection."

"That's very kind of you, Señor Kenyon."

"I would be happy to give you a personal tour. And your friend, too," he added.

"Maybe later," Tyler said.

"Please," he said, extending one of the glasses toward her. "I see you have no champagne."

She pressed her lips together as she looked at the drink. The mere sight of the bubbles was enough to remind her how she'd felt after the last time she'd touched the stuff.

"I'm fine, thank you," she said, "but maybe my friend would like it."

Kenyon's smile dimmed a few watts. "Of course. *Señor?*"

Tyler put his hand on Emily's back. He didn't touch any of the dress this time, only skin. She jerked at the contact. He used her motion to start her forward. "Sorry, but we have to go," he said.

"Nice meeting you, Señor Kenyon," Emily said over her shoulder.

"The pleasure is mine." He lifted the glass in a toast as they moved away. "Enjoy the evening and your stay in Rocama."

Emily could feel Tyler's tension through his hand. She glanced at him once they were out of earshot. "Well, he seems like a friendly man."

"He didn't ask your name."

"He likely didn't have time since you rushed us out of there."

"I think he knew who you are."

She took another look over her shoulder. Kenyon had given his extra champagne glass to a busty young blonde in a black dress. Judging by the smiles they were exchanging, she had probably been his intended target in the first place. "He was being polite. He seemed pretty harmless, unless you think he spiked that champagne."

"Unlikely, but we can't rule anything out. Kenyon's demeanor was too intent. That's what caught my attention first. When he was talking to you, his posture didn't match his words. He came on like he was flirting, but his body language was all wrong. That's why I wanted to get you away."

"Ah, you thought he acted suspiciously. Well, that's good. For a second there I was worried you might be getting all macho and possessive. Caveman stuff. Growling and thumping your chest just because some other guy came up to talk to me."

"And you wouldn't like that?"

"It's a real conversation killer at parties."

"Emily—"

"I know, I know. This isn't a party, and we're not a couple. I don't need another reminder."

He rubbed his thumb along the groove of her spine.

She felt the caress all the way to her toes. She twitched her shoulders to mask her shudder, then had to grab for her evening bag as the strap slipped down her arm. "What are you doing?"

"Maintaining our cover," he said, hitching the strap back into place for her. His fingers trailed down her arm until he settled his hand at the back of her waist. His hand was low enough to touch only fabric this time. It was also low enough for his little finger to rest on the upper curve of her buttocks.

She bumped his hip with hers. "Well, I'm glad to see you're so dedicated to your duty."

"Uh-huh." He steered her toward a less busy area near one of the mirrored walls and stopped beside a potted palm. Not to continue the caress but to switch on his radio transmitter.

Emily listened as Tyler gave a terse report of the encounter with Santiago Kenyon. It sounded as if he were speaking with Chief Esposito, who had remained at their field headquarters to oversee the communications. She didn't agree with Tyler's concern over Kenyon, so she chalked it up to typical Eagle Squadron thoroughness and continued to survey the room as she waited.

For the first time that evening she was able to spot Jack as he glided through the crowd with a tray of hors d'oeuvres. He passed near the envoy, who had moved away from the president and was speaking with a woman Emily recognized as another cabinet minister. Redinger stood a few paces behind them, looking aloof and dashing in a James Bond kind of way. Emily shifted her gaze to the group around the refreshment table just as Duncan arrived there with a fresh bowl of shrimp.

Although they were subtle about it, Emily could see that several women were giving Duncan the once-over. As she'd guessed, even females who belonged to the cream of society weren't immune to the proximity of one of these commandos. When Duncan leaned forward in order to set the bowl down, one woman bumped into another one because she couldn't keep her gaze off his butt.

Tyler finished his radio conversation and lifted his eyebrows in question. "What's the smile for?"

She shook her head, deciding not to explain. Duncan seemed oblivious to the effect he was having. Tyler likely wouldn't notice it, either. "I was thinking that the shrimp looks good," she said.

"There's no reason you can't have something to eat."

"No, thanks. I don't want to risk spilling food on this outfit. Unless you figure the major would spring for the dry cleaning…" She tilted her head, focusing more closely on the woman who'd been bumped. She didn't seem to be paying attention to the other woman's apology, or to the sauce that had dribbled down her yellow skirt when her plate had tipped during the collision. A greasy red stain was already spreading over what appeared to be silk. She ignored Duncan, as well, despite the fact that he was leaning over again to reach past the ice sculpture for an empty platter.

"What is it?" Tyler asked.

"You said Kenyon's body language wasn't right." She

grasped his hand and tugged him forward. "I think I know what you mean. Let's do another circuit around the table."

"What's going on, Emily?"

"I want to get a closer look at the woman in the yellow dress."

"Did you say woman?"

"Yes. She's plump, has white hair and is a few inches taller than El Gato, but the hair could be a wig and she's wearing heels. It's just a gut feeling, but I don't think she's really a woman."

Tyler pulled her to an abrupt halt and relayed what she'd said into his radio. By that time, Duncan was already several yards away. He swung around and propped the empty platter he was carrying beside a round wooden table that held an elaborate flower arrangement. He casually slid one hand into the pocket of his white jacket.

The woman in yellow moved to the other side of the refreshment table, her motions nimble in spite of her surplus weight. She set down her plate and lifted one hand to pat her hair in a purely feminine gesture. Emily could now see her face. It was round, the right shape, and her lips were full, like El Gato's, but her heavy makeup made it difficult to assess her features objectively. It would also cover any possible scar. The lenses of her tortoiseshell glasses glinted in the light from the chandelier, hiding her eyes. Her eyebrows were thicker than average for a woman's, yet not definitive enough to indicate she was a man.

Duncan's lips were moving as he watched the woman. Emily guessed he was asking for a positive identification, but it was impossible for her to know for sure at this distance. "I need to get closer, Tyler."

"No. I won't risk your safety."

Emily wrung her hands. If she was wrong, she would be deeply hurting an innocent woman's feelings. She could force Eagle Squadron to blow their cover for nothing. She glanced toward the envoy and saw that Redinger had placed himself in front of her. Jack and Kurt were approaching them from the far side of the room. The palace guards who had been standing on either side of the entrance were converging on President Gorrell. Evidently the warning had been broadcast over their radios, too.

"Don't overthink this, Emily," Tyler said, squeezing her fingers. "You were right before."

"Yes, but—"

"Trust your instincts. What are they telling you?"

Emily regarded the woman's hands. Her nails appeared to be bare of polish. Considering how dark her lipstick was, the fact that she'd neglected her nails was odd. She wore no rings, and her knuckles were large. An image of El Gato's fist flashed through Emily's mind, and her heart knew the right answer. "Yes," she said. "It's him."

Tyler repeated what she'd said. Duncan moved forward. The woman must have been alert for his approach. Without hesitation, she caught the edge of the table and flipped it on its side.

The shrimp bowl went flying, along with trays of fruit, cheese and elaborate canapés. Plates and cutlery crashed to the floor. The ice sculpture tipped and broke apart, spraying water and chunks of ice. While the other guests stood paralyzed in disbelief, the woman in yellow whipped up her skirt and pulled out a machine gun that had been strapped to her leg.

His leg. Beneath the dress, he wore the dark blue pants of a policeman's uniform.

Emily had no time to draw a breath before she was lying facedown with Tyler flattened over her back. Gunfire erupted. Not just single shots but long, clacking bursts. One of the massive chandeliers crashed to the floor. People screamed. The marble beneath her cheek shook with panicked footsteps. Bullets screeched as they ricocheted around her, sending marble dust and slivers of crystal whistling through the air. She cried out as something stung her arm.

"Everyone get down!" Duncan yelled. He followed with a command in Spanish, but Emily didn't think anyone heard him over the screams and the gunfire. More people were running. One woman was screaming more loudly than the rest. She hadn't run fast enough. El Gato had his arm around her throat and was using her as a shield. The muzzle of his machine gun flashed like a Fourth of July sparkler gone mad as he swept the room.

Tyler slid one arm beneath Emily's waist, straddled her thighs and crawled backward, dragging her with him as far as the potted palm they'd stopped beside earlier. Bullets pinged from the wide, brass planter, knocking loose a shower of dirt and leaves, but the pot was too thick for the rounds to penetrate.

"Curl into a tuck," Tyler said, getting to his knees behind her. "Stay as close to the pot as you can and keep your head down."

She sat up, pulled her knees to her chin and wrapped her arms around her legs, trying to make herself as small as possible. From the shelter of the brass planter, she could see that Duncan had upended the flower table and was crouched behind it. Gonzales was standing behind a pillar. Both had their weapons drawn and trained on El Gato. People who hadn't managed to flee were on the floor. Some were writhing in pain, some were motionless. Crimson glistened on white shirts and jeweled gowns. More crimson streaked the floor and began to gather in pools on the marble.

She trembled. These people could be bleeding to death while she watched. *Oh, God!*

Gonzales shouted in Spanish. Whether it had been a challenge or an order to surrender, El Gato responded by riddling the pillar he stood behind with another burst of gunfire.

"Is the envoy secure, Major?" Tyler asked.

Emily twisted her neck to look across the room. She couldn't see Redinger or Jack anymore, and Helen was nowhere in sight. Neither was the president.

"My bet is he's wearing Kevlar under that dress or he would be down by now," Tyler continued. He spoke with the same measured control she'd heard him use before. "A body shot isn't going to stop him. Duncan?" He paused. "Gonzo?"

El Gato's wig and glasses had come off. His dark hair fell across his forehead. The close-set, reptilian eyes narrowed as he flicked his gaze around the room. He called what sounded like a demand and shoved the muzzle of his gun against the breast of the woman he held. Smoke drifted from the hot barrel. His hostage's screams turned from fear to pain.

Emily sobbed. Everything was happening so fast. This was a nightmare that kept getting worse.

"See if you can get his attention, Duncan," Tyler said. He brought his arms around Emily, pressed close to her back and steadied his gun on the edge of the planter in front of her.

Duncan hung on to the pedestal of the table he was using for shelter and rolled it across the floor a few feet, scrambling to stay behind it.

El Gato swung his gun away from the woman to fire

at Duncan. A stream of bullets shredded the wooden tabletop.

Tyler rested his chin on Emily's shoulder to sight down his gun barrel and squeezed off three shots.

Three holes appeared in the center of El Gato's forehead. His eyes rolled back. He crumpled to the floor like a puppet whose strings had been cut.

The woman who had been his shield staggered aside. Gonzales reached her just as she collapsed in a faint. He caught her beneath the arms and pulled her clear while Duncan kicked the gun away from the fallen assassin.

Emily's ears were ringing from Tyler's shots. She tried to speak, but her voice came out as a croak. She ordered herself to move, to stand, but her body was trembling too badly for her to uncurl from her tuck.

Tyler spun her on her bottom to face him. He cupped her chin to look into her eyes. "Emily, are you okay?" His voice sounded distant, as if he were shouting down a tunnel. He ran his hands over her ankles and up her calves, but stopped short when he reached her elbows. He peeled off his jacket and pulled his shirt from his pants. Then he took a knife from his boot and used it to rip a wide strip of fabric from the bottom of his shirt.

The distress on his face knocked her out of her daze. Only then did she feel the blood that ran down her arm.

Chapter 8

"Our lady will be fine, junior." Jack snapped on a pair of surgical gloves, then swabbed Emily's right arm with disinfectant. "Stop hovering. You're making me nervous."

"She needs a real doctor," Tyler said.

Unperturbed, Jack took a syringe from the tackle box that he used for a med kit. "Then she'll have to wait in line. Best guess, that would mean at least a few hours."

Tyler looked around the ballroom. Though it still was a disaster area, there was order to the chaos. The injured had been triaged by the first emergency personnel to reach the scene. The more critical cases were already being transported to the hospital. Currently, the doctors and paramedics were working their way through the people who remained in order of need. Most of the injuries were gunshots. Some people had suffered broken bones during the panic caused by the shooting. Emily had been hurt by a razor-sharp sliver of crystal from the downed chandelier. It had been kicked up by a stray bullet and was embedded in her upper arm.

As the team's medic, Jack was more than qualified to tend a minor injury like hers. He was right. If he didn't do it, she would have a long, painful wait ahead of her. Yet Tyler felt that she deserved better than being treated in the field like a soldier. He knelt in front of the gilt chair Gonzo had commandeered for Emily earlier and reached for her free hand. "This could leave a scar. Say the word and I'll take you to a hospital. They'll find you a plastic surgeon."

She forced a smile. "It's just my arm. If there's a scar, it will hardly show. Besides, it's only a flesh wound. That's what Jack said. He explained that's what you guys call anything that doesn't involve—" her breath caught as Jack injected a local anaesthetic "—major surgery," she went on. "What kind of wuss would I be if I made a big deal over this scratch?"

He stroked a lock of hair from her cheek and tucked it behind her ear. She'd begun the evening with her curls twisted on top of her head, yet her hair had started to escape the combs and pins long before he'd tackled her and now hung to her shoulders in a wild red cloud. Mascara from the tears she hadn't wanted to acknowledge smudged the skin beneath her eyes. Blood streaked her arm and stained her dress. She'd broken the heel of one of her shoes so she'd taken them both off and was sitting with one bare foot curled over the other.

On the surface, she bore little resemblance to the beautifully dressed woman who had entered this ballroom with him, yet Tyler couldn't get enough of her. He'd had a hell of a time keeping his mind on his job tonight. One look at the way that dress clung to her body had made him remember how he'd first seen her. Naked and magnificent. "You're no wuss, Emily. You're a Valkyrie."

She rolled her eyes. "So I did hear you right. You called me that the day we met."

"It's what came to my mind when I saw you in action."

"Don't they run around wearing scary breastplates and helmets with horns?"

"Only in operas." From the corner of his eye, he saw Jack ready his forceps. "My Grandpa Lindstrom told me they were beautiful warrior women who ride through the air and choose mates to take back to Valhalla with them."

"Well, you're way off base on all counts, cowboy. Besides, I don't ride."

"You could do whatever you put your mind to."

She glanced down at her arm. Her face paled as she watched Jack draw out a three-inch fragment of crystal. He used a gauze pad to absorb the gush of blood that followed. "I can't recall having a splinter that big," she said, her voice rising. "I used to get lots when I was a kid. One of my uncles had an old dock down by the lake and it seemed every time I pulled myself out of the water I ended up wearing part of the boards on my elbows and knees. Stop me anytime. I know I'm babbling. Tell me more about your grandfather. Wasn't he the guy who taught you how to ski?"

Tyler cupped her chin and eased her face back toward his as Jack cleaned out the wound. "Yes. He liked the winters. He liked to brew his own beer, too. Best I ever tasted."

"Sounds like an interesting guy."

"He was. The beer and the long winters were the reasons he was so good at storytelling. Want me to tell you about Thor's hammer?"

"Jack's about to stitch it up and you're trying to distract me, right?"

"Yes. You don't need to watch. He knows if he makes you so much as flinch I'll have to hurt him."

"That goes for me, too," Duncan said, moving past Tyler to stand at Emily's left. "You did well tonight, ma'am. We couldn't have done the job without you."

"I wish I'd spotted El Gato sooner. Then maybe no one would have been hurt."

Duncan rested his hand on the back of her chair. "If you hadn't spotted him, he would have worked his way to the envoy before he opened fire. He could have taken out the president and most of his cabinet, too. We're not the only ones in your debt."

Jack tapped his fingertip against the edge of Emily's wound. When she didn't react, he inserted the tip of the needle into her flesh.

Tyler did his best to keep his own reaction from showing on his face, but he felt every suture as if he were the one getting them.

"Is Helen okay?" Emily asked. "She got away before the shooting started, didn't she?"

"The envoy's fine," Duncan said. "So's the president. The major and the palace guard only needed a few seconds head start, and you gave it to them."

"And the woman who was being held hostage?"

"Shaken up, but unharmed."

She looked past Tyler to the shambles of the ballroom. "How many people…didn't make it?"

The bodies of two women and four men, not counting El Gato, had already been taken away. A few of the critically injured weren't expected to last the night. This wasn't the right time for her to hear the details. "Don't think about it, Emily," Tyler said.

"I can't help it. They thought they were coming to a party. They'd done nothing wrong, any more than the gardener or that poor construction worker. It's not fair. They weren't the assassin's target. They were only in the wrong place at the wrong time."

As Emily had been a week ago. "The important thing is that it's over," he said. "He'll never hurt anyone again."

Her fingers trembled within his. "It's hard to believe how fast the end came."

He guessed from the tremor in her hand that she was remembering the final moments of the standoff. He'd known he would get only one chance to finish it. He wished that he'd had the presence of mind to warn her not to look. "I'm sorry that you had to see that."

"You had no choice, Tyler. You had to kill him. Otherwise, more people would have died. With all the bullets that were flying, it's a miracle that anyone survived. He was shooting everywhere." Her chin trembled. "I can still hear it."

"It'll fade, Emily." He squeezed her hand.

"I was still a little drunk the last time I was shot at. It was already over by the time I got scared, but this..." She looked from him to Duncan and then to Jack. "How do you do it? How can you keep putting yourselves into situations where you know you'll be risking your lives?"

Jack had finished stitching her wound. He spoke for all of them as he smoothed on a bandage. "We think about how much worse it would be if we hadn't been here."

Emily clutched her bag to her chest as she concentrated on putting one foot in front of the other. The walk back to her room had seemed endless, and not only because she was barefoot. Time was playing tricks on her, slowing down or jumping ahead without warning. It was like her pulse. Just when she thought it had settled down, she'd feel another punch of memory and off it went again.

"How's the arm?" Tyler asked.

She tried to shrug, but the tug of the stitches beneath the bandage stopped her. Whatever Jack had used to numb the pain in her arm was wearing off. "Just great. No problem."

"You should try to keep the dressing dry for at least a day."

"Yes, Jack told me. I guess that trip to the beach I'd been hoping for is out. On the other hand, swimming might not be that good an idea, anyway. There are probably sharks in the water. I've heard they're more common in warm regions. What do you think?"

"I think you're wired, and the sooner you get some rest the better you'll feel."

She glanced toward the other end of the corridor. Kurt and Gonzo were back on duty, standing outside Helen's suite. That was no surprise. Even though El Gato was out of the picture, they would continue to act as the envoy's bodyguards until she was safely on her way to the States. The two men gave her a friendly wave, as if there was nothing unusual about the sight of a shoeless woman in a bloodstained evening dress being escorted by a man in a rumpled tuxedo with no shirt.

She focused on Tyler's chest and felt another punch of memory, along with a flutter of sexual awareness that had nothing to do with the danger they'd confronted. Or perhaps it had. The reason he was half-naked beneath that tux was because he had used his shirt to immobilize the crystal fragment in her arm while they'd waited for Jack. He hadn't left her side throughout the whole endless aftermath.

But she wouldn't have expected any less from him. She already knew he was a nice guy. "Thanks for walking me back," she said, opening her door. "And for holding my hand while I got stitched up and all that, but you don't have to feel guilty because I got hurt. It was a fluke."

"I know that." He held out her shoes. He'd been carrying them by the straps so they dangled in midair between them. "Maybe you can get these fixed."

Her eyes filled with tears as she took the shoes from his hand. Seeing the broken heel put the finishing touch on the evening. They weren't glass slippers, that was for sure. And the clock had already struck midnight. This wasn't a fairy tale. People had died tonight.

"What's wrong?" he asked.

"I can't do it."

"Do what?"

"You're probably expecting me to make a crack about whether the major will compensate me for those shoes or my dress. Or I could say something about how President Gorrell won't ask us back to another one of his parties since we did such a bang-up job ruining this one."

"Why would I expect that?"

"Because that's what I always do when I'm trying to deal with feelings I don't like. But I don't need to tell you that. You already figured it out, didn't you?"

He guided her into the room and closed the door. She'd left the lamp on the bedside table burning. It filtered through the rose-colored tulle that framed the bed to create an island of light in the darkness, warm and inviting.

Emily bit her lip as she felt another sexual flutter.

Tyler bypassed the bed and walked to the bathroom. "Stay there," he said. "I'm going to run you a bath."

She dropped her bag and the shoes and followed as far as the doorway. "Why?"

"Because you need to relax." He switched on the lights

above the sink, pushed his jacket sleeves to his elbows and bent over the claw-footed tub.

"You just finished saying I need to keep my bandage dry."

He waited for the water to start steaming, then adjusted the temperature and straightened up. "You can keep your arm on the rim of the tub."

"Oh, great." She leaned her back against the door frame. "Now you're issuing orders again."

"I want to help you."

The tenderness in his tone brought another spurt of tears. She rubbed her face. "Don't feel sorry for me. Just because I'm a bit off my game right now doesn't mean I need your pity. Save it for the real victims of that maniac."

"Of all the things I feel for you, Emily, pity isn't one of them."

"Good. Because it's not a bath that I need."

"Then what? Ask me anything."

"You were touching me all evening. You've hauled me around and knocked me down too many times to count."

"That's true."

"So would it be too much to expect that a guy who seems to have no problem with physical contact might realize I need to be held a lot more than I need a bath?"

He left the water running, walked where she stood and placed his hands on either side of her waist. Taking care not to touch her right arm, he drew her away from the door frame until she leaned against his chest. It was a gentle embrace, compared to what he'd given her in the past. "You'll feel better after you get some sleep."

She turned her face to his neck. "I doubt if that's going to happen. Not unless Jack put more than novocaine in that shot he gave me."

"Your body's still going through the fight-or-flight response. When it wears off, you'll crash."

"It took you a while to calm down after you defused that bomb."

"That's right."

"It's why you kissed me in the stairwell."

"One of the reasons."

"I guess you don't want to kiss me now, huh?"

His grip on her waist tightened. "Emily, if I kiss you, I'm not going to stop until I've stripped off that dress you're barely wearing and whatever racy scraps of lace you've got underneath and tasted every inch of you."

Her heartbeat went off the scale. She curled her fingers around the lapels of his jacket. Her knuckles tingled as they brushed his bare chest. "Doesn't sound like such a bad idea to me. Would it be a problem for you?"

"Damn right, it would. You don't really want me. You just want a distraction. You're not thinking straight, and we both know it."

"What if I don't care?"

"You'll care tomorrow."

"Your mission ends tomorrow."

He rubbed his cheek against the top of her head. "Exactly. I've got enough on my conscience without taking advantage of your mental state. I don't want to give you another reason to hate me."

"Tyler, I don't hate you. I—" She stumbled over the word. What on earth had she been about to say? He was right. She wasn't thinking straight. Being hot for his body was one thing, but she knew better than to let her emotions get involved.

Didn't she?

She kissed his neck.

He straightened his arms, easing her away from him. His chest heaved. "We have to stop."

"Why?"

"For starters, there's the water." He stepped back and leaned down to shut off the taps. He stayed where he was, his hands braced on the rim of the tub. Wisps of steam rose from the surface to wreathe his head. He spoke without looking at her. "I wasn't completely honest earlier."

"Okay. Which time?"

His jaw hardened. "At the reception. When Kenyon was talking to you."

"What about it?"

"I didn't rush you away only because he seemed suspicious."

"Ah."

"You were the most beautiful woman in the room. It didn't matter why we were there, I just wanted you to myself."

She would have cherished the compliment if he hadn't sounded so angry about it. "You seem to think that was a problem, too."

"It was. It is. My duty should be my priority."

Under normal circumstances, she would have accepted the distance he was trying to put between them. She'd pushed people away often enough herself. Instead of admitting that she didn't want to be alone, she'd make a joke or a cynical remark and pretend she didn't need anyone. She didn't risk chasing after any man, because it was so much easier to reject them before they rejected her. Emily didn't wait to be knocked down before she'd come up swinging. That was the pattern of her life.

Yet there already had been a lot of firsts with Tyler. Her relationship with him was unique. There had been nothing normal about it, from the way they had met to the way he kept doing or saying things that slipped right past her defenses. They'd bypassed the preliminaries. They hadn't had time to grow closer gradually. It had simply happened. She *knew* he wouldn't hurt her, and the knowledge was empowering.

She moved behind him and placed her hand on his back. "You're not on duty now, are you?"

"No."

"Help me with my zipper."

He straightened.

"My arm's stiff and I don't think I can manage it myself. You want me to take a bath. I can't very well do it in my clothes."

He turned to face her. The steam had dampened his hair to a dark gold. Moisture dotted his forehead and gleamed at the base of his throat. A vein throbbed in his neck. Without the white shirt to temper it, the black tuxedo jacket that had made him look so handsome earlier now made him look dangerous. It framed the hair on his chest and the swells of muscle above his belt, contrasting the civilized with the primitive. Tendons ridged his forearms as he fisted his hands.

Emily could sense his battle for control and it thrilled her. Challenged her. Keeping her gaze steady on his, she lifted her left arm over her head and turned to expose her side.

The zipper had been sewn into the seam. It was concealed beneath a fold of fabric. Tyler ran his fingers along her side until he found it, then slowly lowered the tab. "What you're feeling is only a reaction to being shot at."

"Then why do I feel it every time you touch me?"

"Emily..."

"Don't stop yet." She moistened her lips. "There's another few inches to go."

The dress began to part. His fingertips brushed the skin at her waist.

"The other side's stuck to me because of the dried blood," she said, lowering her arm. "Could you help me peel it off?"

He dropped his forehead against hers. "Dammit, Emily."

"You say that a lot, Tyler."

"You are the most maddening, contrary, frustrating woman I have ever met."

"Don't blame all of this on me. Why did you walk me back to my room?"

"You were injured. I was worried."

"You could have let Duncan do it. Or Jack."

"You're my responsibility."

"You can protest all you want, but given our history whenever adrenaline is involved, you can't tell me that you didn't have the slightest clue that something like this was going to happen as soon as we got alone."

He rolled his forehead along hers in a slow negative. "I thought I'd be stronger."

"Or maybe you thought I'd be weaker."

"That would have been my first mistake."

She used her left hand to slide the dress off her right shoulder, stopping when it caught on her bandage. "I could use some more help here."

He took her hand, brought it to her side and finished lowering her dress to her waist himself. He inhaled deeply a few times. His breath puffed over her cheek and feathered across the tops of her breasts.

Her nipples tightened instantly, pushing against the black lace teddy that covered them. It had been the only undergarment she'd packed that didn't have straps that would show with her dress. She hadn't planned on anyone seeing it when she'd put it on tonight, but now she was glad that she'd worn it. The clever underwiring gave her cleavage. She guessed by the ragged edge that had crept into Tyler's breathing that he'd noticed the effect, too.

He lifted his hand. He held his palm a quarter inch from the black lace.

"There are hooks down the center," she whispered. "I'm going to need your help with those, too."

He muttered a curse and pulled back to yank off his jacket. He tossed it beside the tub, then grasped the folds of her dress and leaned over to shove it to her feet. As he straightened, he scooped her into his arms. Then he carried her to the bedroom, laid her in the center of the bed and sat on the edge to tug off his boots.

This time, the surge in Emily's pulse wasn't due to a memory. It couldn't have been. Because she'd never experienced anything like Tyler's lovemaking. Once he'd made the decision, he committed to it fully. Enthusiastically. He made short work of the hooks on her teddy. She barely noticed when the rest of their clothes disappeared. But she felt every moment of the pleasure as he joined his body to hers.

He filled her completely. There was no room left in her mind or her heart for anything but sensation. When he began to move, she was ready, oh, so ready, that she trembled around him. The climax came swiftly, neither of them wanting to prolong what they both needed and had waited so long to have.

Yet before Emily could catch her breath, Tyler flipped her over and set about making good on his promise.

He tasted every inch of her.

* * *

"Careful of that arm," Tyler said, reaching past Emily to reposition the towel on the edge of the tub. He lifted her elbow on top of it, then settled her head in the crook of his shoulder.

Now she understood why this tub was so long, Emily thought, snuggling back between Tyler's thighs. It must have been designed with two people in mind. Aside from some delightful crowding, even a six-foot-four hunk managed to fit in here quite nicely.

Being naked with a man in the heat of the moment in order to have sex was one thing, but bathing together was somehow more personal. More intimate. Oddly, Emily felt no shyness with Tyler. She wondered whether it was an aftereffect of adrenaline.

Or it could have been a consequence of the orgasms— the *spectacular orgasms*—he'd just given her. Pretending modesty at this stage would be absurd. She smiled and scooped a handful of water over his knee. "You were right."

"That's good to hear. What about?"

"A bath was a good idea. Why didn't you suggest it earlier?"

He lowered his shoulder so that her head dropped back into the water.

"Hey," she said, coming up dripping. "What did you do that for? Now my hair's going to corkscrew."

He pushed aside a handful of sodden curls and kissed the back of her ear. "I happen to like it when your hair corkscrews. It makes me remember how I first saw you."

"Oh, God. Don't remind me."

He slid his hand over her shoulder and flattened it above her breasts. "I noticed something that morning I've been wondering about."

"Underwire," she muttered.

"What?"

"The reason my boobs looked so perky tonight. I don't want to give you any false hopes."

Laughter rumbled through his chest to her back. He slid both his hands beneath her arms and cupped her breasts to bring them above the water. "These little beauties don't need any enhancement. They are perfect just as they are."

"*Little* beauties? Well, it's all a matter of proportion, you know. On a smaller woman they wouldn't look so—" She gasped as he rolled her nipples between his fingers. "Mmm."

"That's not what I was talking about." He ran his index finger up her breastbone. "I meant the hives on your chest. Was it from the champagne?"

"Oh, that. No, it was from the strawberries."

"Ah."

"I knew I would break out, but they were chocolate-dipped." She lifted his hand to her mouth and licked his fingertips. "I couldn't help myself."

"Sometimes it's tough to keep away from things we want, even though we know there'll be consequences."

She pinched his arm. "Don't start."

"What?"

"Don't think about your duty or your honor or whatever it was that made you try to talk us out of this. I know the mission ends tomorrow."

And I'm going to miss you. I don't want to say good-bye.

She swallowed the words before they could come out. It wasn't love, she reminded herself. "I'm not asking for a commitment. In case you forgot, I'm not exactly the poster girl for lasting relationships. Let's just enjoy the moment."

"I intend to, Emily. Back where I come from, we have a saying about not bothering to close the barn doors after the horse gets out."

"Horse, huh?" She slid her buttocks against his groin. "Well, I wouldn't say that, but I wouldn't call it a *little* beauty, either."

Chuckling, he crossed his arms beneath her breasts. "Once you take your armor off, you're a generous, passionate woman, Emily."

"Only with you, Tyler."

He nuzzled his face against her hair. He didn't respond.

An ugly thought flitted through her mind. Could his initial resistance to sleeping with her have been about more than his job? She should have considered the possibility that someone as gorgeous and as good at sex as Tyler wouldn't lack for women. "You said your sisters are all married."

"Uh-huh."

"Have you ever thought about settling down, too? I started to ask you that before but you never said."

"Yes, I've thought about it. Someday, I'd like to have a marriage like my parents'. They've been together for forty-three years and seem to be more in love every time I visit."

"The only good marriages I saw when I was growing up were the ones in fairy tales. No, on second thought, those stop at 'I do.'"

"My mom and dad didn't have a storybook life. There were plenty of troubles, but they got through them as true partners. They set a good example for all their kids."

"Yet you're still single?"

"Uh-huh."

"There's no special girl waiting for you back in Miller's Hole?"

"I'm unattached, Emily," he said firmly. "Tonight wouldn't have happened if I wasn't, no matter how hard you tried to seduce me."

She pushed the ugly thought back where it belonged. Of course, he wouldn't be cheating on anyone. He was too honorable a man to deceive a woman. She shouldn't let her experience with Christopher's dishonesty taint what she had with Tyler.

"And the truth is," he said, "there's no special girl back home because none of them would have me."

She was surprised into a laugh. "Very funny. A hunk like you? What's the real reason?"

He was silent for a while before he replied. "I had a hard time getting dates when I still lived at home. I was the proverbial runt. It's why I first got into the habit of wearing cowboy boots. I needed every extra inch I could get. I didn't start growing until I was seventeen and then I was as liable to trip over my own feet as my own tongue."

She realized he'd been serious. She tried to picture Tyler as a boy, but it was impossible to get past the image of him as he was now. He was simply too much...man. "I had no idea."

"Being puny in my formative years wasn't my only problem. I was a loner. I preferred the solitude of the range to The Hole and wasn't comfortable doing much talking." He rested his chin on her shoulder. "Things changed when I moved away. Besides filling into my height, I mean. People saw me for what I was instead of what they expected me to be."

"That's when you joined the Olympic biathlon team," she said.

"Right. I had some great coaches. They believed in

training the mind as well as the body. That continued when I joined the army. It gave me skills I'm proud of and the opportunity to be part of the bigger picture."

"You're good at your job."

"It's important to me. It's where I belong."

She took a few moments to digest what he'd said. The self-confidence he displayed now had been hard earned. They had more in common than she'd guessed. Perhaps it wasn't that surprising. Only someone who had experienced repeated rejection would understand the need to develop armor. That's why Tyler *got* her. It was more evidence that the bond they'd developed over the past week went beyond the physical. She rubbed her foot against his calf. "Want to know why I wrote my first newspaper article?"

"You said you were in the ninth grade?"

"Our school's quarterback wanted me to write his English assignments for him. Like an idiot, I'd assumed he had been paying me all that attention because he liked me, but he set me straight. No jock like him would take a second look at a red-headed beanpole. So to save my pride I wrote an article about the systemic cheating that was going on with the entire football team. They all got suspended a week before the regional playoffs."

"Whoa. You had guts."

"Needless to say, that didn't make me Miss Popularity in Packenham Junction."

"I would have liked you."

"I would have liked you, too, Tyler."

He kissed her cheek through her hair. "My family would like you."

"My family would eat you alive."

"That reminds me." He lifted her right arm off the tub rim and turned her so that she faced him. Water sloshed to the tile floor. "I seem to recall you once made a threat about biting."

Emily laughed and opened her mouth for his kiss.

And in that moment, all logic, caution and experience to the contrary, she realized she could far too easily fall in love with a man like Tyler Matheson.

Chapter 9

Black-and-white images were flickering across the monitors in fast-forward as Tyler entered the briefing room. There was another hour to go before sunrise, but Esposito and Duncan were already at work. Or more accurately, judging by the weariness on their faces, they were still at work. He poured a mug of coffee and went to stand behind them. "Are those the surveillance tapes from last night?"

"What's left of them," Esposito replied.

"What happened?"

"According to palace security," Duncan said, "the equipment malfunctioned."

"Sounds too convenient."

"That's what I said." Esposito ejected one tape and started up another. It showed the corridor outside the grand ballroom. The time stamp indicated the footage had been taken two hours before the reception had begun. Figures in catering uniforms moved past purposefully. So did the canine team from the palace guards. "They all cut off ten minutes after the first guests started to arrive."

"Who had access to the security system, Duncan?" Tyler asked.

"In that section of the palace, the feed was split between the regular police force and Gorrell's guards." His jaw worked as he suppressed a yawn. "I already showed them how to tweak the setup so it can't happen again."

"You figure El Gato had help from the police?"

"He had to. We didn't find any stripped cop in the area, or any chubby woman missing her dress. That means he didn't play it by ear by acquiring his disguise once he got in. This was planned beforehand."

Esposito rubbed his face. Stubble rasped under his palm until he moved his hand to his bald pate. "Gorrell's got some more housecleaning to do. Someone on the inside is playing on the other team."

"Did anything come back on those security checks your pals reran, Dunk?" Tyler asked

"The staff all checked out. We're still waiting for more background on some of the politicians. Oh, and we did get an ID on the prints we sent them from El Gato's body. His real name is Miguel Castillo. He's originally from Rocama. Used to work for the Juarez family as an enforcer before he tried his hand at freelance work and went international."

"Which means he'd have connections all over the island. Any one of them could be the one who helped him get past security."

"Yeah. We can't relax our watch on the envoy. There could be more trouble to come."

"Let me know if anything pops up from Intelligence." Esposito got off his stool and stretched. "I'm going to catch a few hours' sleep before the major's briefing."

"Sure thing, Chief."

He looked at the mug that Tyler held. "Careful with that stuff. It's been cooking all night."

Duncan waited until Esposito's footsteps had faded, then swiveled to face Tyler. He regarded him in silence.

Tyler set the coffee down without tasting it. "You got something you want to say to me, Duncan?"

"What's the point? I'm not your keeper. I'm not hers, either."

There was no reason to ask whom he was referring to. Kurt and Gonzo had seen him go into Emily's room. They'd also seen what time he'd left. Word traveled fast among the team. It wouldn't take a trained observer to put the pieces together.

Tyler wasn't going to make any excuses. For one thing, what had happened between him and Emily wasn't anyone else's business but theirs. For another, he had enjoyed it too much to pretend he was sorry. Making love with her had been inevitable. Though the timing had been bad, he couldn't honestly regret the act. Or acts. He only hoped that eventually, she would feel the same way.

He checked his watch, then emptied his mug and put on a fresh pot of coffee. He watched as the coffeemaker burbled. "Any meetings on the envoy's schedule before she leaves?"

"Only one. It's the payoff."

"Why?"

"Seems she got what she wanted. Gorrell's going to sign the deal for the base."

Tyler turned, surprised. "When did that happen?"

"There were some midnight phone calls while you were busy. The incident with El Gato knocked most of the president's cabinet off the fence. The general consensus was that any group who has the capability to get an assassin through palace security and stage a direct attack is a serious threat to the government itself. They realize they need help to stop the Juarez cartel."

"Politicians can see the advantage of having a powerful friend."

"The annual rent for the base won't hurt, either. The cartel won't find it so easy to buy support once we move in."

"The major must be pleased," Tyler said. "I heard he's been wanting to finish the job against the Juarez family for seven years."

"Uh-huh. Looks like everyone got what they wanted last night."

It was the second swipe. "I thought you had nothing to say."

"Hell, Tyler. Emily was hanging on by a thread after Jack finished with her. We all saw that. You were supposed to be the one who was concerned with her feelings."

"I was and I still am, Duncan."

"She's earned our respect. She deserved better."

Tyler fought to hang on to his temper. He wasn't going to let Duncan provoke him, because he would need all his resources for the battle that was yet to come. It was the only one that really counted.

He'd told the major he would see his duty with Emily through to the end. Now that the envoy was going to get her deal, it appeared the end had arrived.

"You're right about one thing," Tyler said. "Emily did deserve better, but you're wrong about the other." He poured a fresh mug of coffee and walked to the door. "I didn't get what I wanted. Not by a long shot."

Emily lay on her back and listened to the distant rumble of thunder. The stars had disappeared behind a bank of clouds hours ago, so the only way to judge the time was from the gradual lightening of the gloom. She wasn't sure whether she'd slept after Tyler had left, yet she didn't feel fatigued. She felt energized. All she needed was to think about the things they'd done together and an echo of pleasure went zinging through her body. If she felt any shame, it was because an evening that had ended so tragically for others had ended so perfectly for her.

Well, not quite perfectly. Perfect would have been waking up to see Tyler's face on the pillow beside hers. She moved her arm to the place where he'd lain. His warmth had faded hours ago. She rolled to her side and pressed her face to the sheet. Only a trace of his scent remained. She closed her eyes and inhaled what there was of it, then flopped onto her back again and draped her arm over her face. "Damn," she whispered. "You've got it bad."

So much for not letting her emotions get involved. She'd almost convinced herself that it was going to be strictly sex. After all, any healthy woman would have had a hard time remaining physically unaffected by a man like Tyler.

Yet as much as he'd pleased her physically, it was his words that had made the deepest impact. It took a very secure man to admit his vulnerabilities. It also took a secure man to admit that he did want a stable, loving partnership for life. That wasn't fashionable for most guys. There was still a double standard in society. Men, particularly handsome, sexy ones, were expected to play the field and to avoid commitment like the plague. Yet Tyler had spoken readily about admiring his parents' marriage. It amazed her that no woman had snagged him before this.

Not that she could consider him snagged now. One night of sex, especially an incomplete one with a whole truckload of extenuating circumstances, did not a relationship make. She'd been the one to say she wasn't expecting a commitment. She knew full well that she shouldn't let her imagination get away from her. She needed to be cautious. She was still on the rebound from the most disastrous relationship of her life. Her judgment was impaired.

Yet if she wasn't already half in love with Tyler, it wouldn't take much to push her the rest of the way over the edge.

As if on cue, there was a gentle rap on her door. Emily rolled off the bed and drew on her robe. She winced when the sleeve caught on the edge of her bandage, but she'd already dismissed the pain before she'd crossed the room. She knew of only one person who would seek her out at this hour. She also felt as if she could sense his presence.

She stopped to take a steadying breath before she touched the doorknob. Sensed his presence? God, she did have it bad. She fluffed her hair, pulled her robe closed and tied the belt.

"Emily?"

Tyler's low voice sent another one of those pleasant zings through her body. She reminded herself to at least attempt to keep her cool. She didn't have too much experience with morning-afters, and she'd had no experience whatsoever with mornings after nights like the one she'd just had. How was she supposed to act cool when the thought of seeing him again was already making her melt?

She opened the door.

"Good morning." He held up a mug of coffee. The aroma drifted across the threshold like a spiced kiss. "It's not as good as Chief Esposito's but it should do the job. Can I come in?"

Oh, yes. She was teetering right on the brink. She closed the door behind him and went to turn on the bedside light. He'd showered and shaved. His hair was still damp and rumpled by his typical finger-combing. He was wearing his jeans and a blue golf shirt instead of a suit. It reminded her that the mission would be ending today.

Some of her pleasure dimmed. "Thanks, Tyler." She took the mug from his fingers. "I could use some coffee."

He glanced around the room. Instead of going to the bed, he walked to the window seat.

The clouds beyond the window flashed with lightning. Emily tried to ignore the chill she felt as she moved toward him. It was probably the weather. "What I'd really like is a good-morning kiss."

He cradled her face in his palms and gave her a long, thorough kiss. Yet when she pressed closer, he caught her elbow and stepped back. "We need to talk, Emily."

"What's wrong?"

A volley of rain hit the windowsill and drummed on the notebook she'd left on the seat. Tyler shut the window, drew the curtains closed, then picked up her notebook and moved it to the floor, along with her stack of printouts and her camera. "Please, sit down."

"If you're getting delayed conscience pangs about whether or not you took advantage of me, just forget them. I thought we got that settled."

"No, this concerns something else. I need to clear the air." He took her hand and guided her to the cushion. "Please, sit. This may take a while."

She did as he asked because her legs were beginning to feel wobbly. "You're making me nervous, Tyler. My experience with morning-afters is pretty limited, but I don't think they're supposed to go like this."

"I'm sorry. I realize I should have discussed this before we slept together, but once I touched you I couldn't bring myself to stop."

Emily raised the mug of coffee to her lips to give herself something to do with her hands. "I'm not going to get pregnant," she said against the rim. "I had just finished..." She cleared her throat. "It was the wrong time of the month."

He looked startled. "Damn. I can't believe I hadn't even considered that. What an ass I am. I never thought to bring a condom."

"One wouldn't have been enough anyway, but it sounds as if that's not what's on your mind, either. I could play this guessing game all morning and not get it right, so you might as well just say it before I end up telling you more stuff you didn't really need to know or spilling this coffee all over myself."

He sat beside her and cupped her shoulders. "What I want to talk about has absolutely nothing to do with you and me, or what we did last night. It's about our mission."

That was the last thing she'd expected. She gulped a mouthful of coffee and set the mug on the windowsill. "What about it?"

"Now that El Gato's dead, the reasons we brought you into the mission are over. We don't need you to identify him, and he's no longer a threat to your safety."

"Okay. That's good, isn't it?"

"Yes. I've heard that the Rocaman government has agreed to the proposed base, too."

"So the mission was a success."

"Right."

"That's great."

He didn't look like a man whose mission was coming to a successful close. His expression was growing grimmer by the second. "You made a deal with Major Redinger. You'd give us your help in exchange for our cooperation with your story."

"Ah, and now that you don't need my help, you don't want me to feel obligated to hang around anymore, is that it? Well, I don't mind tagging along while you do whatever it is you do to finish up after Helen leaves. It would give me the chance to get some closing quotes for my article."

"There can't be an article, Emily."

"Oh, no. I have plenty of material." She gestured to her notebook. "Enough to stretch it into a whole series if someone buys it."

"There's no easy way to say this." He took both of her hands between his. "We can't allow you to publish anything about us or our work here. It would create political difficulties for President Gorrell. It would also compromise our safety on subsequent missions."

It took a few beats for his words to register. She shook her head fast. She couldn't have heard him correctly. "No, you're mistaken. The major and I had an agreement. I said I'd hold off trying to sell my story only until your mission was over."

"You can never publish it, Emily. Not our names, our backgrounds, our photos or any details about our actions. The special ops teams like Eagle Squadron have to remain anonymous."

"But—"

"It's standard operating procedure. It's why there was no record in the papers of what we did the last time we were in Rocama."

"No, this time's different. Redinger agreed."

"He needed your cooperation. To keep the mission confidential he felt he had no choice but to agree to your demands."

"But it was his suggestion to embed me with the team. You're making it sound as if he knew all along he wasn't going to keep his word."

Tyler regarded their joined hands. More rain hit the window. The curtains did little to muffle the sound. "He was concerned that you would alert the media to our presence here before our mission was finished. He wanted to keep you close."

"Keep me close," she repeated. "Under surveillance, you mean. So it wasn't my imagination. You didn't trust me. You were supervising me. That's why you were restricting my movements."

"I was also protecting you."

"My God, I saw it but I didn't put it together. That's why there's no phone in this room. That's why the guards at the palace gates had orders to stop me from going out." She tugged her hands but he hung on. She shifted her legs so they no longer touched his. "What about all those interviews? What about the talks we had?"

"Emily—"

"I told you how much this article means to me. I thought you understood. I thought you sympathized."

"I do understand, and I'm sorry we had to deceive you."

"Why are you telling me now? Because you slept with me?"

"El Gato is dead and the envoy's deal's going through, so there's no justification for continuing the charade. You have the right to know the truth. And yes, also because I slept with you."

Her head was whirling. She felt as if she were back on one of those hangover carnival rides, only there was no merciful fuzziness to dull her brain. She looked at the stack of printouts she'd brought back from the library, then at the notebook she'd carried everywhere with her for a week. She thought of the meticulous notes, the hours of work, the days of excitement over undertaking a project so ambitious.

It couldn't have all been for nothing, could it?

Yet Tyler had called it a charade.

She jerked out of his grasp and got to her feet. "I need this article, Tyler. It's my ticket to a new life. I need the money. I need..." *I need to believe in myself.*

That's what she'd hoped to gain, more than the money or the career boost. She'd needed to believe in her future and find some way to heal her pride. She'd wanted something to hope for, to look forward to. Something that would let her regain the control she'd lost when she'd given her love to Christopher. She'd wanted a new dream to replace the one that had been shattered when she'd trusted the wrong man.

Just as she'd trusted Tyler.

Oh, good God! She'd done it again.

He stood and reached for her. "I'm sorry."

She smacked his arm aside and backed away. "When did you find out the deal was a fraud, Tyler? It was obviously before last night." More thoughts surfaced from the whirl in her head. "That's why your conscience was bothering you. Because you knew you'd been lying about everything."

"Not everything."

"When did you know? Tell me. Before you kissed me the first time? Before you let me cry on your shoulder about the last man I trusted?"

"I knew from the first day, Emily."

She clutched her robe closed at her throat. Suddenly, she felt too exposed. "And the other men?"

"They all knew."

"Then those interviews, the quotes I got and the notes I took, it was all a farce. You were just going through the motions to keep me happy."

His jaw twitched. He nodded.

"I don't suppose it occurred to anyone to simply tell me the truth?"

"You agreed to cooperate only if we gave you our

story. We couldn't be certain how you would react if we refused. Then once we started, we had to continue. Try to understand, our priority had to be our mission."

"Of course, it was. You've warned me often enough, only I never had the presence of mind to put all the pieces together. You used me. You duped me." She forced a laugh because she'd be damned if she'd cry. "You're men. You'd think I'd learn."

"We knew it wasn't fair to you, but we wanted you to be safe."

"And you wanted your mission to be successful. Well, it was. Your charade paid off. Congratulations." She turned her back and started for the door. "You all must be very proud of yourselves. Message delivered. Now get the hell out of my room."

He caught her before she'd taken three steps, sliding his arms around her waist and pulling her back to his chest. "You have every right to be angry, but please, hear me out."

She fisted her right hand, covered it with her left and drove her elbow backward. Tyler's breath whooshed out as she caught him hard in the ribs, but he didn't loosen his hold. "Take your hands off me," she said.

"I realize you're upset."

"Upset?" She strained to free herself. The stitches in her arm stretched warningly but she didn't care. "No, Tyler. Upset doesn't begin to cover it. I'd give you a thesaurus so you could look up a few more appropriate words but if I had something that solid in my hand I'd be apt to turn it sideways and shove it up your—"

"Emily, for God's sake, listen to me." He lifted her off her feet and somehow managed to twirl her in midair to face him. He clasped her tightly, fitting the curves of her body into the angles of his. "There'll be other stories. You're intelligent and perceptive, and you've got an exceptional talent with words. You'll find another subject that's going to take you wherever you want to go."

"Put me down," she said through her teeth.

"I can't. Not yet. Give me a chance."

"How stupid do you think I am? No, don't answer that. It's obvious, because only a total idiot would let herself get used the way I did. Twice. I sure don't learn, do I? I came to Rocama to get away from the train wreck I'd made of my life and I stepped right into another." She blinked furiously. She was *not* going to cry. "But at least I didn't waste a year on you, only a week."

"The only thing I deceived you about was your article. I've been honest about everything else."

"Right. Sure. Given how thoroughly you had me snowed about my work, I'd be an absolute fool to trust what you say about anything else."

His gaze bored into hers. "Then try trusting what I did. You can trust how we felt when we made love."

Her heart contracted as if she'd been punched. She pulled her hand free from his embrace and slapped him. "Don't you dare call it that."

He didn't flinch at her blow. When she lifted her hand for another, he turned his head and kissed her palm. "Hit me all you want if it makes you feel better. It doesn't change how I feel."

Even now, there was a part of her that wanted to believe him. She touched her fingertips to his cheek, unconsciously caressing the place that she'd struck.

"What we have is special, Emily."

"We have nothing, Tyler. It was all an illusion. I saw what I wanted to see, just as I did with Christopher."

"No! It's not the same."

"How? You both lied. You both used me to further your

own agenda. The only difference is you actually got to enjoy the wardrobe that I'd bought to wear for him."

He kissed her. It was hard and possessive. So was his embrace. Passion flowed from his touch, mingling with the anger that streamed from hers until it was impossible to distinguish the two. Fury flipped to desire, propelling her even farther away from reason.

Sobbing, she grabbed his hair between her fingers and held on tight while she kissed him back. He'd lied. She should hate him. Yet she knew what his touch could do and responded despite herself. Her breasts were already swelling. Heat rushed through her core so fast it made her wince.

He must have been as attuned to her body as she was to his. He slid his hands beneath her robe and dug his fingers into her naked buttocks. One twist of his wrists and her hips aligned intimately with his. His grip was strong enough to bruise, yet the pain only drove her pulse faster. She hooked her legs around his waist and clung to him.

"Emily." His voice was hoarse, as breathless as she felt. Beneath the denim of his jeans, she could feel him harden. He shifted his grasp to her waist and lifted her until her breasts were level with his face. He closed his lips around one nipple and drew it, robe and all, into his mouth.

The friction of his tongue through the silk, the pressure of his erection against her inner thighs, was enough to make her shatter. She groaned and threw back her head, helpless to stop the wave of release that ambushed her body.

Yet when it finally ebbed, she didn't feel fulfilled, as she had before. She felt empty. And sadder than she'd ever been in her life. The joy she'd experienced the night before had been tarnished. She'd been cheated out of far more than her story.

"You have to know I never lied about this," he whispered.

He licked the valley between her breasts. "What's going on between us is real."

She let go of his hair so she could wipe her eyes. She wouldn't listen to him. He'd betrayed her, and now her own needs were betraying her. How could she have let him—

No, she hadn't *let* him. There hadn't been any question of permission or choice, any more than she could have chosen not to be angry. "Yes, it's real. It's lust. Is that what you were trying to prove with this little demonstration?"

He slid her down the front of his body until her feet touched the floor. "It's more than lust."

She breathed deeply and prayed that her voice wouldn't crack. "You were right yesterday. I didn't really want you. I just wanted a distraction. Amazing what a dose of that good ol' adrenaline can bring on. I suppose I should thank you. This interlude was marginally more enjoyable than slamming my fist into your face, which is what would have happened if you hadn't distracted me."

"Don't."

Was that pain in his voice? Or was she weaving yet another pathetic fantasy around a man she'd thought she was in love with?

No. She was not in love. She might have thought she could be, but she'd come to her senses. She wasn't that much of a fool. "There's no reason to candy-coat what you and I did simply to help ease your conscience. Or mine."

"Emily—"

"We had sex, Tyler, plain and simple. Since it's not going to happen again, there's no reason for you to hang around." She braced her palms on his chest and shoved backward.

This time, he let her go.

A rumble of thunder vibrated through the floor. Its echoes died slowly, leaving the room silent save for the drumming of the rain and the harsh rasp of their breathing.

Emily straightened her robe. The silk that Tyler had moistened with his mouth slid coolly across her breast. She shook with the effort not to cry. "Go away."

"We'll talk later."

"No. I don't want to talk to you, I don't want to touch you, and I don't want to see you."

He lifted his hand to her cheek. "We can't leave it like this."

She jerked her head to avoid any contact. "There's nothing left between us. Our professional relationship was a farce from the beginning and our personal relationship is over." She went to the door and wrenched it open. "I'm sure you have some pressing duty you need to perform elsewhere, so don't let me keep you."

"Emily, I'm sorry."

"Goodbye, Sergeant Matheson."

He remained where he was.

"What do I need to do to get through to you? Just leave!"

He returned to the window seat and picked up her notebook from the floor. He retrieved her camera from the top of the stacked library printouts, then walked past her and paused. His jaw was rigid. "I am sorry, Emily," he repeated. "But I have to take these with me."

She slammed the door. The impact echoed through the walls with a boom that rivaled the thunder.

Emily decided it was reply enough.

Chapter 10

Dawn broke watery and gray and got bleaker as the morning progressed. The stones in the courtyard glistened almost black. The flowers were furled, leaving only masses of dark green over the sodden soil. Unrelenting rain drummed on the window. Emily was fine with that. She wasn't in the mood for sunshine. She moved woodenly around the room as she packed her belongings, taking care to remove every trace of her presence. She put on her most comfortable dress, which happened to be the one with the bullet hole in the hem. That was fine, too. It would serve as a good reminder of what could happen when she lowered her guard. Keeping her gaze away from the bed, she buttoned her cardigan, closed the door to her room for the last time, then wheeled her suitcase down the corridor as far as the envoy's suite.

Major Redinger was talking quietly with Jack as they stood outside the door. The major was in full ribbons-

and-medals uniform this morning, looking as crisp as the first time she'd seen him. Though both men greeted Emily politely, neither one looked her directly in the eye.

She wasn't surprised. She was well aware of how tight the team was, and she'd assumed that Tyler would have informed them that he'd revealed the truth about the charade to her. He'd also likely told them it hadn't gone well. That was good. Then she wouldn't need to explain what she was about to do. She drew a folded piece of paper from her purse and held it out. "I'm glad to find you here, Major Redinger. This is for you."

Redinger didn't make a move to take the paper. "I'm afraid I don't have much time, Miss Wright. I'm on my way to the garage. We need to prepare the convoy to the airport."

"Thank you for the update, but your schedule or that of your men is of no further interest to me."

It was hard to decipher the expression on the major's face. As usual, his granite features gave nothing away. Not even an apology. "I understand that you're disappointed in the way we secured your help, but it was the best option for everyone concerned. I hope you can take some satisfaction in how valuable a contribution you made to our mission."

The anger she'd been nursing rekindled. Once again, she welcomed it, because it was far better than the pain. These men had made a fool of her, but if they thought she was going to hide meekly in her room until they had left, they were sorely mistaken.

She knew how to look out for herself. She'd had years of practice. They were going to pay for the damage they'd done, just as they had a week ago when Tyler had crashed through her balcony doors. She had come full circle. Her vacation was going to end almost as it had started. She snapped her wrist to unfold the paper. "Speaking of valuable contributions, this is a list of what Eagle Squadron owes me."

Redinger looked at his watch, then took the paper from her hand and began to read it aloud. "'Item one: digital camera plus memory card.'" He glanced at Jack. "Was it erased?"

"Yes, sir. Sergeant Colbert already saw to it."

He took a pen from a pocket inside his jacket and crossed out the first line on the paper. "We'll return your camera."

Emily clutched her hands together to keep them steady. She had known the pictures of the men would be deleted. They would never be published. It was pathetic to have wished she could have kept some of them for herself. "Send it over to the Royal Rocaman Hotel. I'll be staying there until my flight leaves tomorrow."

"Done." The major resumed reading. "'Item two: one designer evening dress. Item three: one pair of gold leather heels.'"

"Those articles were damaged beyond repair, so I expect to be fully reimbursed. I've listed the original cost."

He cocked one eyebrow as he looked at the amount, then continued. "You state here that item four is an estimate for future medical bills."

"I'll need to see a doctor to take the stitches out of my arm. Since I'm unemployed, I have no medical insurance."

Jack stepped to her right and touched his fingertips to the outline of the bandage on her upper arm. "You should let me check this before you go."

She refused to consider the suggestion, even though she'd found fresh blood seeping from the stitches after Tyler had left. The wound had reopened, so it was almost certain that she'd have a scar. Still, the one she'd have on her arm was nothing compared to the one she'd have in her heart.

She lifted her chin. She wouldn't let herself wallow. She'd done enough of that after Christopher. She really had to get on with her life. Yes, indeed. She should be used to the routine by now. She didn't need a man. She didn't need love, and she sure as hell wasn't going to trust her feelings when it came to either one again. "My role in your mission is complete, Sergeant Norton, so my welfare is no longer your concern."

"I'll see that you're reimbursed for any treatment you need," Redinger said. He slipped his pen back into his pocket and offered her a business card. "Send the bills to me."

She stuffed the card into her purse. "As you can see, item five is my return airfare. I've included that because my entire holiday was monopolized by your mission, so I shouldn't be expected to pay for the trip myself. I doubt if you soldiers do."

"No, we don't. We use military transport."

"Then we're agreed?"

He nodded.

"The final item is the bill for my time. I used the salary I was making at my previous job as a base rate and calculated overtime at the standard time-and-a-half for evenings and for the weekend I worked. I believe the amount is fair."

Redinger folded the paper. "Yes, it's fair," he said. "You functioned as part of the team on this job and you should be compensated. Was there anything else?"

His easy acquiescence threw her for a moment. Part of her had been hoping for a fight. "Yes. There's the matter of a possible reward."

"I'm not sure I follow you."

"El Gato was an international assassin, known to Interpol

as well as countless other law enforcement agencies. It's reasonable to assume someone was offering a reward for his capture. Since I was instrumental in identifying him, I believe I deserve a portion of any funds that might be available."

"If there was any reward," the major said, "the palace guards would be collecting it."

"And why is that?"

"They're being given the credit for stopping his shooting spree. Officially, we were never at the reception."

She blinked. She'd thought she would be getting over it by now, but it continued to get harder to keep her eyes from filling. The men had erased more than her pictures. They were rewriting everything that had taken place, as if last night had never happened.

But she should want to forget last night. "Of course. How naive of me."

"The palace sent out a press release with the official version an hour ago," Redinger said.

A press release. It was the final insult. While she'd worked for a week on the real story, she'd been scooped by a piece of fiction. Her temper snapped. She fisted her hands on her hips and glared from one man to the other. "Well, well. It seems that Eagle Squadron doesn't have the only skilled liars around here."

"Miss Wright—"

"I'm impressed that you both managed to shave this morning. But then, with enough practice I suppose you don't have any trouble facing yourselves in the mirror. Step aside, please."

Jack shifted closer and put his hand on her left shoulder. "Emily, I'm sorry. Once you calm down, you'll see that—"

"I'm going to speak to Ms. Haggerty. We have an interview."

Neither one of them moved.

Emily grasped the handle of her suitcase, wheeled it over the toes of Jack's shoes and knocked on the door. "Don't worry. The envoy will be perfectly safe with me. She is, after all, a woman."

Tyler spread a cloth over the plank he'd propped on a pair of paint cans, opened the ammo box and counted out enough shells to fill his spare magazines. One by one, he cleaned them off before he inserted them, his fingers moving nimbly through the task he'd done countless times before. He'd already disassembled and thoroughly cleaned his pistol, as well as the submachine gun he'd be bringing along on the convoy. Normally, it helped focus his mind.

Not today. He slipped the full magazines into his pockets and secured the box. With the right weapon, he could hit a moving target at a thousand yards with no problem. He had defused every kind of bomb except a nuclear one. He knew more about munitions than any other man on the team.

Yet when it came to Emily, he'd handled her feelings with all the finesse of a drunk wielding a pellet rifle.

He glanced at the notebook that lay on his duffel bag, then reached to pick it up. His thumb rubbed along the groove that bisected the front cover. The crease had happened when Emily had dropped it on the stairs the first time they'd kissed. The lower right corner was filled with her cross-hatched doodling, one of her habits when she was bored. The center was marred by raised dots from the raindrops that had hit it this morning. It was a testament to the past nine days in more than words.

He should have destroyed this notebook as soon as he'd

brought it upstairs. Those had been the major's orders. But he hadn't been able to bring himself to let go of it yet. There was too much of Emily in these pages.

Tyler opened the notebook to the section toward the back that she'd marked with a dog-eared fold. Her handwriting was full of sharp angles and big loops, too full of energy to be contained within the lines. It slanted forward, reflecting the same headlong courage Emily displayed in the rest of her behavior. At places, she'd pressed her pen hard enough that he could feel the outline of the letters through the paper. He could hear her voice as soon as he read the first paragraph of her unfinished article.

My Week with Our Secret Warriors
by Emily Wright
The Caribbean island nation of Rocama may seem like a tropical paradise, yet beneath the beauty an unseen battle for dominance is being waged between the Juarez drug cartel and the democratically elected government of Norberto Gorrell. America has sent their best, a team of Delta Force commandos known as Eagle Squadron, to help ensure the country remains in the hands of the people. Though these dedicated soldiers are willing to put their lives on the line, they expect no recognition....

She had crossed out a few lines after that. Tyler could tell by the number of strokes she'd used that she'd been dissatisfied with the way the words had gone. He flipped backward to her notes. She'd organized pages for each member of the team, jotting down points that they'd given her during their interviews, along with her own comments. Many of her observations had impressed him with their accuracy. He regarded her bullet-point summary.

Viktor Gonzales, known as Gonzo—Cuban father,
Danish mother. Gung-ho attitude, rule-follower.
Jack Norton—medic, newly engaged but still edgy.
Rule-bender.
Mitchell Redinger—widower with ring. Career army.
By-the-book hard ass.

Tyler smiled at her terse description of the major. He could picture the tight set of her mouth as she wrote the words. Emily might have been fast-talked by Redinger initially, but she hadn't been intimidated by him. Not much daunted her. She would have been a force to contend with if she'd ever decided to pursue a military career. He turned to another page.

Kurt Lang—mechanical genius. Prefers machines
to most people.
Duncan Colbert—overachiever. Very intelligent,
likes to analyze.
Tyler Matheson—strong family ties. Sensitive, com-
passionate, controlled. Impressive sense of duty.
Honorable. Off-the-scale gorgeous...

His smiled faded. His entry in her notebook took up several pages and was by far the largest. Emily had jotted down every scrap of background information he'd given her, much of which he'd forgotten he'd said. She had written those words before he'd told her the truth. If she had the chance now, she would likely cross out most of it. Her pen wouldn't only leave grooves, it would go through the paper.

It gave him no satisfaction to see that she liked the way he looked. She'd never pretended that she didn't. She'd have to be attracted to him in order to want to have sex.

Was that really all it had been for her?

He'd known her for just over a week, yet he felt as if he'd known her for years. He realized much of that was due to her emotional state when they had met. She'd needed someone to confide in, and he'd had plenty of experience listening. Naturally, they'd grown closer. Their near-constant physical proximity had accelerated the process.

He'd always known he would end up hurting her. It had given him an extra urgency to make the most of the time they did have. It was why he hadn't been able to deny himself the chance to make love to her, even though he'd known there would be a reckoning.

Damn, he was a selfish bastard. He'd realized Emily had an issue with trust, and as he'd guessed, the team's deception had made it worse. What would have happened if he'd gone against the major's orders and told her the truth earlier? For starters, she wouldn't have felt used and betrayed. She might have realized that he wasn't anything like Christopher. They might have had a chance to let their relationship develop naturally and see where it went...

Or she might have walked out on the mission and straight into a bullet from El Gato.

Tyler exhaled hard, then swore and closed Emily's notebook. Should he have done anything differently? That was another one of those questions with no right answer.

The sitting room of the envoy's suite reminded Emily of the one she'd seen on the ground floor when she'd first been brought to the palace. It had the same lush plants, the same peach and dark wood color scheme, only it had a tall window like the one in her room instead of terrace doors. A gust of wind rattled the panes. Emily suppressed a shiver. "The rain's not letting up," she said. "I hope the weather doesn't delay your flight."

"It's the meeting beforehand that I'm more concerned with. I hope no one begs off because of the storm." Helen picked up the silver coffeepot from the low table in front of the couch where they were sitting and gestured toward Emily's cup. "More coffee, dear?"

Emily covered the top of her cup with her hand. "Oh, no thank you. I've already had more caffeine than I should."

"I noticed that you appeared tense when you arrived. If there's anything you want to talk about, I'm an excellent listener." She poured an extra inch of coffee in her own cup and set the pot on the tray with their empty lunch dishes. "It's one of the requirements for my job."

Emily smiled, which was something she'd doubted she could have done two hours ago. She was far less tense now than she'd been earlier. Focusing on her work had been what she'd needed. The envoy had answered all her questions about the future American base in Rocama with patience and candor. She'd also shared some fascinating stories of her years in the diplomatic corps, as well as her childhood as an army brat. It was everything Emily could have hoped for and more. "I'd much rather talk about you."

"We've been doing that for the past two hours, and quite frankly, I've run out."

"I'm sorry. I've been monopolizing your time." Emily capped her pen and set it on top of the notepaper she'd borrowed from Helen. She'd tried to keep her writing as small as possible, but she'd filled both sides of nearly every page. "It was very kind of you to have me join you for lunch when you must have dozens of details still to take care of."

Helen tapped her knee before she could stand. "Don't concern yourself. My work here is almost done, and I can't recall an interview I've enjoyed more. You're refreshingly direct. I could tell by your questions that you're meticulous about accuracy."

"Thank you."

"I'm sure you're going to go far as a journalist, Emily. And if there's anything I can do for you in the future, please, don't hesitate to call me."

"I appreciate that, Helen. Be careful, I likely will."

"It wasn't an idle offer. I owe you my life."

"Really, you don't—"

"And I'm also feeling guilty," Helen said, holding up her hand.

"You? Why?"

"I heard how you were tricked into joining the mission."

Emily suspected she'd probably heard the noise of the slamming door this morning, too. "It wasn't your doing."

"No, but I suspected something days ago. It seemed odd to me from the beginning that Major Redinger would have allowed a reporter such free access to his team. Delta Force soldiers are normally very secretive."

"Yes, I'd known they were, too. It's one of the reasons I was so excited about the opportunity to get their story. I should have realized when something seems too good to be true, it usually is."

"I can't begin to tell you the number of times I've needed to remind myself of that very point during negotiations. It's difficult to stay objective when we desire something strongly."

It was true, Emily thought. She hadn't looked too closely at her deal with the major because she'd wanted it so badly. She'd done the same thing with Christopher. She'd wanted to be loved and had closed her eyes to anything else. "You're right. My eagerness made me gullible. It's why I was so thoroughly scammed."

"Yet because of the deception, you were in a position to save my life yesterday." Helen smiled. "Forgive me if I can't completely disapprove of what you call the scam."

Emily fidgeted with the hole in her dress hem. It was impossible to disagree with Helen's logic. Yesterday, Tyler had mentioned being part of the bigger picture. Was this an example of what he'd meant? "It was Eagle Squadron who saved your life, not me."

"Now who's being diplomatic?"

"Really, all I did was point El Gato out. The soldiers did the rest."

"They reacted swiftly."

"Thank God for that."

"That's why military men tend to be more goal-oriented than the rest of us. Soldiers have to put their duty first when they're on a mission. Lives depend on their decisions. They're often called upon to make difficult choices."

Emily was aware of what Helen was doing. As gently as possible, she was lobbying on Eagle Squadron's behalf. She was doing an effective job, too. "In my head, I do know that. My resentment of them must seem petty to you."

"No, dear, it's human. Your pride was hurt. Once you have some time to put this experience into perspective, I'm sure your resentment will fade."

"Talking with you has helped a lot, Helen."

"Good. I admire everyone who has the courage to serve in our armed forces, yet believe me, I also know how frustrating it can be at times to deal with the military mind-set."

"That's for sure."

"Especially when one's emotions become involved. More than your pride was hurt, wasn't it?" Helen asked.

"It's…complicated."

"Because of Sergeant Matheson?"

Emily hesitated. "I'm not sure what you mean."

Helen regarded her over the rims of her glasses. "I wouldn't be much good at my profession if I wasn't able to pick up on certain undercurrents. You two seem to have become rather close over the course of the past week."

Emily's eyes misted without warning. She folded the sheets of notepaper and leaned down to slip them into her purse. She couldn't think about Tyler without getting a lump in her throat. She hoped she would be able to put her experience with him into perspective someday, too.

Yes, far more than her pride was hurt when it came to Tyler. She'd warned herself often enough that she should have been more cautious. Luckily, they'd only spent one night together. Once they went their separate ways, there would be no ties left between them. No legal matters to worry about, no small-town gossip to brave, no I-told-you-sos from her family. So, looking at the big picture, it could have been far worse.

"If we seemed close, it was because of the mission," she said, smoothing a fold in her dress so that the bullet hole didn't show. "But we always knew it was going to end."

Chapter 11

It was hard to hear the radio over the rain. Tyler covered his ear with his palm to block out the background noise as he left the garage. "Say again, Jack?"

"She left the envoy's suite five minutes ago. She's on her way down."

He lowered his head and increased his pace. "Gonzo, do you see her?"

"She just passed me. Nearly ran me over with her suitcase."

"Where?"

"Ground floor. She was heading toward the portrait gallery."

A limousine glided in front of Tyler as it circled toward the parking area beside the rear gates. He dodged to the side to let it go by, then broke into a jog. The members of President Gorrell's cabinet were beginning to arrive. Though some of them had dragged their feet about the base for a week, they were all making sure they showed up on the winning side now.

"The meeting's scheduled to start in thirty minutes," Jack said. "We'll be bringing the envoy down in twenty."

"Check."

"The major wants us all there, junior."

Tyler's footsteps echoed from the walls as he ran beneath the arched carriageway. He'd need to change into his suit before he could join the team. It would take him several more minutes to get to the conference room where the envoy's final meeting would be held. But first, he was going to talk to Emily. Once she left the palace, who knew when he would get another chance? "I'll be off the air for fifteen. Cover for me, Jack."

"Sounds like you're planning on having radio trouble."

"Yeah."

"I hope you know what you're doing, kid."

"So do I," he muttered. He switched off his radio, tucked his earbud into his pocket and headed across the inner courtyard. He reached the double doors to the portrait gallery just as one was pushed open.

Emily paused on the threshold to unfurl an umbrella. She was concentrating on the locking mechanism and didn't see him until she looked up. For an instant, a spark of pleasure lit her eyes but it was quickly doused. "Tyler," she said.

He grasped the shaft of the umbrella handle to keep her from moving outside. "Where are you going?"

She looked pointedly at the suitcase behind her, then tugged at the umbrella. "I'm leaving."

"Your flight isn't until tomorrow."

"I'm leaving the palace. I'm going back to the hotel

where I can have a phone and room service. I am free to go now that I'm of no further use, right?"

"I can't stop you, but I would like to talk to you."

"There's nothing more to say, other than goodbye."

He slid his hand down the handle until he touched her fingers. "Please, Emily. You can spare me a few minutes, can't you?"

Her cheek flexed, as if she were biting the inside of it. She dropped her hand, then shoved her suitcase backward and stepped aside to make room for him to pass.

Tyler closed the umbrella and propped it against the wall. The door swung shut behind him, cutting off the noise of the rain. Water dripped from his hair and drizzled down his cheeks, and he thought about how twelve hours ago he and Emily had been sharing a bath.

She drew the edges of her cardigan together. "You're all wet."

"I was at the garage with Kurt. We're preparing the cars we'll use in the convoy."

"Oh, right. The major mentioned that."

"How's your arm?"

"Fine."

"Did you get your interview with the envoy?"

"Yes. She was very gracious."

"That's great."

"And who knows, I might be able to publish this one."

"How many times do you want me to apologize, Emily?"

She turned her back to him and moved over to stand in front of the nearest painting. It was a portrait of a swarthy man in what was probably eighteenth-century finery, but she likely hadn't noticed. She was looking at the floor instead of the canvas. "It's okay, Tyler. That was my last jab. I've pretty well spent my anger. I realize you were only doing what you had to do."

"I'll always regret that we had to lie."

"We saved a life. Our country's getting a base on Rocama."

"But we hurt you."

She lifted one shoulder. "I didn't get what I thought I would, but I've made a good connection with an influential diplomat. The major's going to compensate me for my time. Overall, I'm better off than I was when I got here."

She was saying all the right things. He should be happy that she'd calmed down enough to be reasonable. But her shoulders were curled, as if she had drawn in on herself. And her voice was too quiet. He would have preferred her to yell some more. It would have meant there was still some passion left.

He moved behind her. "I've been thinking about what you said this morning."

She laughed. It was hollow and devoid of humor. "I said a lot. I was blowing off steam. I got carried away. I realize you might find it hard to believe, considering how even-tempered and docile I usually am, but I tend to over-dramatize things from time to time."

"You said our personal relationship was over."

"It was probably an exaggeration to call it that. How much of a personal relationship could we have? We've only known each other a week."

"Nine days. Emily, please look at me."

She didn't move. "We met under exceptional circumstances. Things got intense. There's really not much more to it."

"We slept together. I can't be casual about that."

"People have sex all the time. That's why there are so many people. It wasn't that big a deal. It's just that I've never done a one-night stand before so I didn't handle it as well as I might have."

"It doesn't have to be only one night. I'd like to see you again once we get home."

She shook her head.

He'd realized this wouldn't be easy, not with a woman as stubborn as Emily. He should be patient, but the fifteen-minute window he'd asked the guys to give him was evaporating fast. He took her by the shoulders and turned her to face him...and felt his heart turn over.

She'd kept her shoulders curled so that he wouldn't notice her trembling. She'd spoken softly so that he wouldn't hear the catch in her voice. She hadn't wanted him to see her tears.

Tyler passed his thumb over her cheeks. "You don't want to end this any more than I do, Emily. Otherwise, you wouldn't be crying."

"No, Tyler. I'm sad because I realized from the start there could be nothing between us."

"Why not?"

"I have a life to put back together. I have a career to build. There's also a certain scuzzball's trial I'm going to testify at. Have you forgotten that this trip was supposed to be my honeymoon?" She lifted her left arm to wipe her eyes on her sleeve. "I knew all along this wasn't the right time for me to think about getting involved with another man."

"Then when?"

"When what?"

"When will you think about it? In a month? Three months? Three years?"

"I can't put a timetable on how I feel. That's not something anyone can schedule."

"I agree. Feelings don't have a timetable. Mine didn't.

After only nine days, I feel closer to you than I've felt to anyone in my life."

She drew in a ragged breath, then walked past him to where she'd left her suitcase. "It was the circumstances, Tyler. Don't make this goodbye harder than it has to be. You're a nice man, and I won't pretend that I didn't enjoy most of the time we spent together, but if you're looking for more, I'm the wrong woman."

He fisted his hands in frustration. If he went over there and pulled her into his arms, he was sure he could make her respond, but that wouldn't solve anything. It hadn't before. "I'm not Christopher."

"We had this conversation already."

"We started it, but we didn't finish it. You're pushing me away because of what he did to you, not what I did."

She curled her fingers around the handle of her suitcase. She didn't reply.

"You're fixing all your armor back into place because you're worried about making another mistake."

"Yes, I am. Only a fool doesn't learn from them."

"Giving up isn't the solution."

"Who's giving up? Didn't you hear me? I'm going to build my career and put my life back together."

"I meant giving up on us."

"There is no 'us.' You really haven't been listening."

"I've been listening to what you haven't said, Emily. We both know you've got a problem with trust. You claim it's because you can't trust men, but the truth is, you don't want to trust yourself."

She faced him. "Bingo."

"But you can, Emily. Your instincts are good."

"What happened this week proves they're not. I was angry that I was duped, and yes, I took it out on you and the guys, but I know damn well that I was the one really at fault. That's why I was so furious. I can't trust my judgment when it comes to my feelings, which is why there's no future for us."

"I won't believe that. We have a bond. You must have felt it."

Her eyes gleamed with a fresh spurt of tears. "Maybe you were only seeing what you wanted to see, too, Tyler. Did you ever think of that?"

Her words hung in the air between them. And for a crucial instant, he hesitated.

The doors to the courtyard swung open, sending rain gusting across the threshold. A pair of palace guards strode inside. They were followed by a short man in a long black raincoat. Three more guards brought up the rear.

Emily wiped her face quickly and rolled her suitcase back to let the men pass, but the short man halted abruptly when he saw her and Tyler. He stepped closer to Emily, switched the briefcase he carried to his left hand and sketched an affected bow with his right. "Hello, beautiful *señorita*," he said. "What an unexpected surprise."

It was Santiago Kenyon, Tyler realized, the oily minister of culture they'd met the night before. He was probably on his way to the envoy's meeting, along with the rest of Gorrell's cabinet. It was odd that he would try to get to the conference room through the portrait gallery. Taking five guards along with him was overkill, too. Maybe it suited his ego. He had to have a giant-size one not to realize he was interrupting a private conversation.

Tyler stepped to the side to go around the guards and started toward Emily.

At a snap of Kenyon's fingers, they blocked his path.

Tyler glanced at them impatiently. "Relax. I'm with the envoy's bodyguard detail," he said. "I've got clearance."

When they didn't respond, he repeated the same thing in Spanish.

Kenyon set down his briefcase, caught Emily's elbow and nodded to the guards. "Take his weapons."

Tyler shifted his weight to the balls of his feet and held his arms loosely at his sides, automatically assuming a combat stance. He didn't draw his pistol because he wouldn't want to risk any stray bullets in such close quarters, but the guards had to realize he couldn't let them disarm him. "Easy now. There's obviously a misunderstanding here."

"Oh, there's no misunderstanding at all, Sergeant Matheson," Kenyon said. "I know exactly who you are. You're the man who killed Miguel Castillo. Please, give my men your weapons before our lovely Miss Wright gets hurt."

It seemed to happen in slow motion. Or maybe everything seemed fuzzy because of the tears that still blurred her eyes. Emily watched in horror as the guards closest to Tyler grabbed his arms and slammed him against the wall.

"No!" she yelled, lunging forward. "Stop!"

Kenyon changed his grip from her elbow to her arm and yanked her back to his side. His fingers dug into her bandage.

The pain stunned her. Emily staggered and fought to catch her breath.

Tyler pivoted on one foot and whipped the trailing leg in an arc toward the guard on his left. His boot connected with the man's jaw, snapping his head to the side. As the first guard crumpled to the floor, Tyler had already driven his elbow into the windpipe of the second.

The other three men were on him immediately. Emily's stomach rolled at the sound of their fists hitting Tyler's flesh. "Stop it!" she cried. "Why are you doing this? He's not your enemy!"

"You're wrong, *señorita,*" Kenyon said. "Tell him to surrender."

Tyler closed his hand over the fist of one of his attackers and twisted him backward. There was a noise like a stick snapping. Or a bone breaking. The man screamed and stumbled into one of the paintings. The heavy gilt frame broke apart as it crashed to the floor, sending pieces of wood skidding in every direction. One of the largest ones bounced against Emily's feet.

She didn't stop to think. Nothing was making sense, anyway. So she stooped fast, grabbed the piece of frame in her left hand and swung backward at Kenyon.

He must have ducked. The wood hit the wall instead. Before she could draw it back to try again it was twisted out of her hand. She felt something cold press against her neck.

"Enough!" Kenyon ordered. "Tell him to surrender or I will be forced to slit your throat."

From the corner of her eye, Emily saw the gleam of a metal knife blade. She looked at Tyler. He had downed the fourth man and had the fifth in a choke hold. Despite the overwhelming odds that had been against him, he was seconds away from overpowering all of his attackers. Whatever was going on here, she knew she would be better off with Tyler than with Kenyon. She gritted her teeth and said nothing.

"Matheson!" Kenyon called. "Release my man now or she dies."

Tyler looked up. The instant of inattention cost him. One of the fallen guards hooked his hand around Tyler's ankle and pulled him to the floor. Another knelt on his chest and pressed a gun to his temple.

Emily screamed. "No! Don't shoot."

Tyler glared at Kenyon. "If you hurt her, I will kill you."

"That is an idle threat from a man whose life I could end with a snap of my fingers," Kenyon said. He slid the blade along Emily's throat until the tip pressed against the skin beneath her ear. "But I believe you'll both be more use to me alive. For now," he added.

Emily held herself as motionless as she could. She hardly dared to breathe. What on earth was going on? Kenyon was in President Gorrell's cabinet. Why was he threatening her and Tyler? Why were he and these palace guards behaving like thugs?

Only, they weren't palace guards, she realized, moving her gaze from one face to another as the rest of the men slowly got back to their feet. She'd seen countless members of the president's elite guard unit over the course of her week in the palace, yet she'd never seen any of these men. She glanced up and down the gallery, but it remained deserted. Surely not everyone in the palace could be in the conference room already.

Kenyon barked a series of orders. The men turned Tyler over and searched him for weapons. They pulled a pistol from the small of his back and another one from a holster on his ankle. They had missed the knife he kept in his boot, Emily realized, yet what good would a knife do against guns? He wouldn't get the chance to use it anyway. They locked his wrists together behind his back with a pair of handcuffs and levered him to his feet. An instant later, her own arms were seized and forced behind her while her wrists were handcuffed.

Handcuffs? Emily thought. Were they police?

"How much is the Juarez cartel paying you, Kenyon?" Tyler demanded.

"I am gaining far more than wealth, Sergeant Matheson, but I don't expect a mere soldier to understand that."

"You've got enough to buy these guards," he said.

"They're not real palace guards," Emily said. "I've never seen any of them before."

"Yeah. I figured they were fakes from the way they fought. A real guard wouldn't have gone down that easily."

One of the men was holding his right arm against his chest. It was probably broken. He stepped forward and gave Tyler a backhanded blow with his left, but at a signal from Kenyon, he retreated.

"Miss Wright has a talent for faces, doesn't she?" Kenyon said. "She's the one who spotted Miguel."

"Who's Miguel?" Emily asked. She wanted to draw their attention off Tyler before they could hurt him further, but it was no use. He spoke again, anyway.

"Miguel Castillo is El Gato's real name," Tyler said. "It wasn't in the press release. Only someone working for the cartel would know that. We suspected they might have someone in the government."

"I've had a long and profitable business association with the Juarez family," Kenyon said. "But you, Sergeant Matheson, have made this personal." He caught Emily's chin and turned her face toward his. "And you, too, beautiful *señorita*. You see, Miguel was not only a fighter for our cause, he was my cousin."

Emily met his gaze and did her best to keep her fear from showing. She'd noticed the strong resemblance between Kenyon and El Gato yesterday. They had the same coloring, the same body shape and size. They even moved in the same way. Yet she'd never suspected they could be related.

Oh, God. Now what?

"I knew you had been brought into Eagle Squadron's mission in order to identify Miguel," Kenyon continued. "I thought to turn the tables by identifying you for him."

"I don't understand."

"Come now. Why do you suppose I would have approached you at the reception? I was pointing out where you were so he could avoid you." He squeezed her jaw hard between his thumb and fingers. "But you found him, didn't you?"

"Your beef is with me, Kenyon," Tyler said. "I killed him. She didn't even want to be there. You're taking a hell of a chance coming back to the palace just to get revenge."

"Revenge?" He dropped his hand. "No, I'm here for the envoy's meeting. Encountering the two of you is simply a—" He paused, as if searching for the right word. "A bonus," he finished. He crouched in front of the briefcase that he'd set on the floor earlier and opened the lid.

There were no papers or files inside the briefcase. No computer or phone or any other tool a politician might normally bring to a meeting. The interior was filled with blocks of a white substance that looked like modeling clay connected by a tangle of colored wires to a circuit board and what appeared to be a timer.

Emily looked at Tyler. Like her, he had a clear view of the briefcase's contents. One glimpse of his expression and her suspicion was confirmed.

It was a bomb.

Thunder rolled beyond the walls, like the echo of a distant explosion. Emily clenched her jaw to keep her teeth from chattering.

"You've got nothing to gain with that device, Kenyon," Tyler said. "It's over. The deal for the base is going to go through, whether the envoy is alive or not."

"There will be no base if no one is left in the government to sign the deal," Kenyon said, stroking a blunt-tipped finger along the edge of one of the white blocks. "Isn't it obliging of the envoy to gather everyone in the same place for me?"

Emily's stomach lurched. "Oh, my God. You're going to the meeting so that you can kill them all."

"If I must. I'd prefer to give the president the chance to resign first, to minimize any international repercussions. The rest of our people are already moving into position throughout the palace to ensure the transition goes smoothly. Once Gorrell steps down, I will assume control. If he refuses, he will die and I will assume control. Either way, the end result is the same."

"You're talking about a coup," Tyler said.

Kenyon smiled. "We prefer to regard it as returning Rocama to the way it was before your country saw fit to interfere in our nation's business."

"There's no way you're going to succeed. After the attack yesterday, the security is tighter than ever."

"Palace security has never posed a problem for a member of the government. Particularly now that you've presented me with the perfect delivery method for my ultimatum." Kenyon focused on Emily. "I believe Miguel would have enjoyed having you present my handiwork. It will have a certain artistic irony."

"You can't really expect me to help you," she said. "You're a bunch of thugs."

"Leave her alone," Tyler said. "She's a civilian. She's not part of this."

"Everyone has their price. In this case, she already revealed it." Kenyon nodded his chin toward the guard with the broken arm. He struck Tyler again, opening a split in his lower lip. Blood trickled from his mouth. Another man stepped up and gave him a series of hard blows to his ribs.

"Stop!" Emily begged. "Please, stop!"

The second guard placed the muzzle of his pistol against Tyler's ear.

"No!" Emily cried.

"Do as I say and I will let him live," Kenyon said.

"Don't listen to him," Tyler said. "He hasn't thought this plan through. It's a desperation move. Hang tight and we'll be fine."

Kenyon gestured to his man. "Shoot him."

Emily jerked forward. *"No!"*

"It's up to you, Miss Wright."

As far as making deals went, these men were the last ones she could trust. Yet how could she stand by and do nothing while Tyler was killed before her eyes? As long as he was alive, there had to be hope, even if she only bought him a few more minutes.

She'd told him she didn't want him in her life. She'd been about to leave him. It had seemed the best choice at the time, the safe and sensible one, yet suddenly, all her fretting about trust and judgment and making mistakes seemed ridiculous. What did any of that matter? The possibility of losing him forever was tearing open her heart as surely as that bomb would rip apart their bodies.

No. She couldn't let her mind go there. Not if she was going to function.

She'd wanted perspective. Well, she should be careful what she wished for, because seeing Tyler with a gun to his head sure knocked her feelings into focus in a hurry. "I'm sorry, Tyler."

"It'll be all right. You shouldn't get involved."

"No, I mean about what I said to you before they came.

I'm sorry." She looked at Kenyon. "Okay. If you want me to carry it, I will."

Tyler strained against his handcuffs. "Emily, no! Keep out of this. It's not your fight."

"My dear *señorita,* you will not be carrying it." Kenyon slipped his hands beneath the bomb and gently lifted it from the briefcase. "You will be wearing it."

Chapter 12

Emily didn't know how she was still able to stand. The blocks of C4 that were taped around her waist had been getting heavier with each minute that had passed. Or had it been hours? She had no way of knowing. The muscles in her shoulders were screaming and her hands were going numb from the handcuffs. Her body was trembling so badly, her legs were threatening to collapse. Kenyon's grip on her elbow was all that was keeping her upright.

Gunfire sounded from somewhere beyond the conference room walls. It had been going on all afternoon, but it wasn't something Emily could get used to. She cringed reflexively.

"Hang in there," Tyler murmured. "You're doing great."

She glanced over her shoulder. He was too far away for her to touch or to smell, so she clung to the comfort of his voice. The split on his lip had stopped bleeding, though his left eye was purpling and beginning to swell shut from a blow he'd received the last time he'd attempted to move toward her. As if making sure he didn't try again, one of Kenyon's thugs jerked him sideways and pressed his gun to the base of Tyler's skull.

Emily faced the front of the room again and blinked to clear her vision. None of Kenyon's men were pointing a weapon at her. They didn't need to. They knew as long as they had Tyler she would do exactly as they said.

"I am losing patience, Norberto," Kenyon said. He brandished the remote detonator in his hand. His thumb was poised above the switch that would activate the bomb's timer. "There is only one choice for you to make. Resign now. My men are already securing the palace while I speak."

"You underestimate my people, Santiago," Gorrell said. "They are true patriots, not guns-for-hire or corrupt police. Give up now and I will allow you to live."

Emily curled her nails into her palms and fought to stay upright. The standoff showed no sign of ending. President Gorrell was right. Kenyon had badly underestimated the determination of the Rocaman government. He'd assumed everyone would plead for mercy as soon as they saw Emily walk into the room with the bomb.

They hadn't. Although the handful of palace guards who had been stationed along the walls had laid down their weapons on Gorrell's orders, not one of the politicians who were seated around the mahogany table in the center of the room had tried to flee or to dive for cover. Like their president, they were counting on the loyalty of their people to prevent the coup.

Similarly, if Helen was afraid, she was covering it well. She sat stoically beside the president, her expression closer to indignation than fear. Major Redinger stood behind her chair, looking as solid as a rock. Gonzo stood three paces to her right. The rest of the team had been stationed in the corridor. They, too, had surrendered their weapons to Kenyon's men when they'd seen the bomb Emily wore. That aspect of his strategy had worked as he'd expected.

Would things have been able to progress this far if she'd refused to help Kenyon? Or would Tyler be dead now instead of standing behind her?

It had been a split-second decision, similar to those that soldiers had to make. It had given her yet another new perspective to chew on, whether she needed it or not.

Kenyon squeezed her arm and tugged her to his left, farther away from Tyler. She glanced behind her. Despite the split lip, the blackening eye and the gun to his head, he gave her one of his almost-smiles.

Warmth flowed through her body, lending her strength she hadn't realized she still had. The decision she made now wasn't a split-second one. It had been building in her heart for days. She was in love with Tyler. Totally. Thoroughly. No doubts about it, she loved him. And it sure didn't have anything to do with the way he looked.

Great. Wonderful. So she'd finally worked through her insecurities enough to admit she was in love. Fat lot of good that did her now. Why couldn't she have figured it out earlier? She could trust her feelings about Tyler. He had proven what kind of man he was over and over through his actions. He'd deceived her only because he'd wanted to save a life. Two lives. Even though he'd been torn about it, he'd done his duty, he'd honored his principles. In fact, he wouldn't be the man she loved if he *hadn't* deceived her.

What a mess.

A spate of automatic gunfire sounded from directly outside the room. The doors shuddered as they were struck, but no bullets penetrated the thick wood.

"It is over, Santiago." President Gorrell pushed back his chair and stood. "Your people have failed."

"No. It is you who are finished. The last of your resistance has been eliminated."

The gunfire stopped suddenly. One of the guards near Gorrell stepped forward to speak into his ear. The president smiled. "My troops confirm it. You stand alone now, Santiago. Tell your men to put down their weapons."

"Your bluff will not work."

"It is no bluff." Gorrell lifted his hand. As one, the Palace Guards retrieved the weapons they'd dropped earlier and aimed them at Kenyon. "We have no wish for further bloodshed," Gorrell said. "And I don't believe these men you've brought with you were paid enough to martyr themselves."

Emily sensed a subtle shifting among the thugs who stood around Kenyon. She waited, hardly daring to breathe. Oh, please, please. Let it be over.

Kenyon yanked Emily closer to the doors. His fingers pressed cruelly into her bandage. A shaft of agony made her legs buckle.

"No!" Tyler yelled. He dived forward and hit the floor in front of her as she dropped. With his shackled hands as useless as hers, he had only his body to cushion her fall. She landed on her knees and toppled sideways. Tyler twisted himself so that her shoulder hit his back. Her heart stopped until she realized that the bomb was safely untouched between them.

The endless waiting was over.

Everything happened all at once after that. The bullet-studded doors burst open. More palace guards moved swiftly into the room. From the corner of her vision, Emily saw Gonzales take aim at the man who had been holding

Tyler while the major vaulted over the conference table and closed in on Kenyon.

The palace guards opened fire. Bullets whizzed over her head. Kenyon staggered backward.

"Get the detonator!" Tyler shouted, rising to his knees.

Kenyon was already down by the time Redinger reached him. His hands were empty. Redinger turned him over. "He fell on it."

Tyler twisted to look at Emily. "I need my tools."

Jack and Kurt appeared beside him, submachine guns slung over their suit jackets. While Kurt helped Tyler to stand, Jack relayed his request into his radio. "The chief's on his way down with the box, junior," he said.

"That's going to take too long." He jiggled his cuffed hands behind him. "Who's got the keys?" he demanded.

Gonzo stooped over the body of the man who'd held Tyler, patted his pockets and withdrew the keys to their handcuffs. He tossed them to Jack, who unfastened Tyler's first, then Emily's.

The major gripped Emily gently beneath her arms and lifted her to her feet. "Where do you want to work, Sergeant?"

"The table," Tyler said. "I'll need the room cleared, Major."

"Done. Gonzales, Lang, stay with the envoy."

While Helen and the politicians were ushered outside, Redinger guided Emily to the mahogany conference table. "Just slide up here, Miss Wright," he said. "This is almost over."

With Jack's help, Emily hitched herself up on the table. Any relief she might have felt at the end of the standoff was rapidly seeping away. "Uh, Tyler?"

He leaned over to take his knife out of his boot, slid a chair in front of her and sat. "You'll be okay, Emily."

"You're cutting the bomb off. That's what's going on, right?"

"I can't do that yet. I need to disarm it first."

"Tyler?"

He lifted his knife to her midriff and finally met her gaze. Though his features were tightly controlled, he couldn't hide the emotions that roiled in his eyes. There was worry. Fear. And a fierceness that stole her breath.

She took another look around the rapidly emptying room. The bodies of Kenyon and his men were being dragged unceremoniously outside. Within seconds, no one else was left, except her and the remaining men from Eagle Squadron. They were regarding her almost as fiercely as Tyler. She glanced down.

The timer beneath her right breast was alight with blinking red numbers. "Oh, no."

He fell on it.

The significance of the major's words finally registered. Kenyon's last act had been to activate the bomb, whether he'd intended to or not.

Tyler braced his forearm against her thigh. "I need you to keep as still as possible, okay?"

She started to nod, then bit her lip.

"You can do this, Emily."

"Sure. No problem. Um, how much time do we have? I didn't want to look."

"Three minutes, forty seconds."

The numbers were meaningless. Her brain couldn't process the measurement. She flattened her hands on the table and straightened her arms slowly in an effort to keep herself steady.

"How does it look, Matheson?" the major asked.

"Kenyon knew his way around explosives," Tyler replied, inserting the tip of his knife beneath a black wire. "I watched him rig a secondary circuit when he taped this on. It'll trigger the charge if I tamper with it."

"That's an unusual skill set for a politician."

"He was El Gato's cousin." Tyler pried the wire loose. The numbers kept counting down. "Looks as if he calculated just enough time to get clear when he set the timer. The rest of you need to leave now."

He wanted them safe, Emily realized. Just as he'd wanted her at a safe distance the last time he'd defused a bomb. She looked at the familiar faces around her. During her stay with them, she'd come to know these men almost as well as she knew Tyler. This could be the last time she saw them. Or him.

Oh, God, she didn't want to die. "You can stop it, can't you, Tyler?"

"I can't stop the timer, so I'm going to interrupt the firing train."

"And that will do it?"

"Sergeant Matheson is the best ordnance man in the service," Redinger said as he walked to the door. "You've got nothing to worry about, ma'am."

"Beer's on me when you're done, junior," Duncan said as he followed the major.

Jack was right behind him. "Hey, Dunk, if you've got money for beer, you can afford to pay up what you owe me."

"No way. You rigged that last bet."

"What do you mean? I gave you five-to-one odds."

The banter continued as the men moved into the corridor. Their voices cut off when they closed the doors behind them.

Emily knew what they were doing. She'd tried to lighten

the mood often enough herself when what she'd really wanted to do was cry or scream. She wished she could think of something light to say now, but fear was clogging her throat. She lifted one hand from the table and reached out to touch Tyler's hair. "Is there anything I can do to help?"

"Sure." He pressed his chest against her knees so he could bring his face closer to the bomb. "Try not to move."

She dropped her arm to her side. "I'm sorry."

"Your touch felt good. It always does. I just need to keep my hands steady."

"I'm sorry how we left things earlier. Before...this happened."

"It doesn't matter now." He grasped another wire between his fingers and twisted it away from the timer. "Save your energy."

For what? she wondered, feeling a bubble of hysteria rise in her throat. She'd told him there was no future for them. She hadn't meant it literally. "Tyler, can you really keep this bomb from exploding?"

"I'm doing my damnedest."

"Because if you have any doubts, I want you to be sensible and leave."

"I can't do that."

She watched the numbers flick downward. Three minutes. Her breath hitched. "The other men did."

He set down his knife and used both hands to ease a cord from between two of the blocks of C4. "I'm not going anywhere without you, Emily."

"I realize this is your job, but—"

"Do you really want to argue now?"

"Well, yes, because you're being so damned stubborn with this noble, protective thing you've got going."

"For the past two hours I've been going out of my mind waiting for the chance to pry you away from this thing. I kept thinking that if I had let you leave the palace when you'd wanted to, you would have been gone by the time Kenyon got here. Right now you'd have been safely at the Royal Rocaman, enjoying some room service and a telephone."

"If I had really wanted to go, you wouldn't have been able to stop me."

Something shifted against her waist. The timer gave a sharp beep.

"Tyler?"

"It's the backup fuse. You didn't want to go? You seemed pretty determined to me."

"In my head, sure. But in here…" She pressed her palm to her chest. "No."

Moisture beaded on his upper lip. He pulled out another wire.

"I don't want to give up, Tyler. I do want to see you again."

"This could be adrenaline talking, Emily."

"Gee, ya think? Adrenaline? I suppose it's possible, seeing as how I'm sitting on a table with a bomb strapped to my body and a timer blinking away what could be the final seconds of our lives and— Oh, God, it's down to two minutes. The clock is fast. It has to be."

"You shouldn't have let Kenyon put this on you."

"Don't lecture me now, Tyler. I couldn't watch them kill you."

"Kenyon wouldn't have killed me or he would have lost his hold over you."

"I couldn't take that chance. I love you."

He withdrew his hand from the bomb. His fingers were shaking.

"Okay, I realize this isn't the best time to tell you this, but my options are kind of limited right now and I wanted you to hear it just in case...well, you know."

"Dammit, Emily."

"There you go again. You're always saying that. Not that I blame you. I've been an emotional wreck from the time you met me. A scared and self-indulgent mess. But what I feel for you is too strong for me to doubt. It's got to be. Because I'm terrified out of my wits at the prospect of dying, yet all I can think of is how I don't want to lose you."

"You won't."

"And I'm still not expecting any promises or commitments. They wouldn't mean much, considering that you're sort of under duress here. I only hope if we get through this, you'll still want to give our relationship another try. You were right, we do have a bond. When you're near me, I can feel you even when you're not touching me. And when we're apart, just the thought of you fills up this empty space inside me that I hadn't realized was there." She licked at a tear that trickled into her mouth. She hadn't realized that she was crying again. "You're a part of me, Tyler. I love you."

He sat back and rubbed his face hard, then took a deep breath and focused on his hands. They were still trembling. "The most important job of my life," he muttered. "And I'm shaking like a leaf."

"Uh, maybe it would be better if I stop talking."

"Emily, if we live to be a hundred, I don't think that's going to happen."

"Tyler..."

He stood and caught her face between his hands. "But even if we have only one more minute, I swear to you there's no one else in the world I'd rather spend it with."

The timer gave another beep. Emily inhaled sharply. "Tyler!"

He retrieved his knife and sliced through a trio of wires.

The red numbers went to zero.

Emily squeezed her eyes shut and held her breath.

But there was no blast. No noise. No pain. Only the warmth of Tyler's lips as he settled his mouth over hers.

She blinked and pulled back. "It didn't go off. We're still here."

He slid his knife blade beneath the duct tape that held the explosives to her waist, peeled the bomb from her body and laid it on the table. Then he braced his hands on either side of her to cage her between his arms. His gaze was no less fierce than when he'd first begun to work. "Did you mean what you said?"

"Which part?"

"The part about loving me."

How could terror flip to joy so quickly? She touched the split in his lip, then feathered her fingertips over the swelling above his eye. "With all my soul, Tyler."

He turned his face against her hand and inhaled deeply. When he looked at her again, his eyes were moist. "I love you, Emily."

She could feel the truth of what he said in his voice, in his touch, and in the cascade of memories that blurred across her mind. She'd spent her life yearning to be loved. This time, she knew it was real.

He clasped her hips and pulled her to the edge of the table.

Emily lifted her arms and opened her heart, welcoming Tyler into both.

Pink-tinged sunlight crept across the market plaza. The cobblestones still glistened, washed clean by yesterday's storm. The sounds of dogs and seagulls drifted across the hotel balcony where Emily was standing, along with snatches of conversations in half a dozen languages. News of the attempted coup had spread quickly, and the world's press had begun arriving the night before. Emily counted no less than four television news crews and at least a dozen reporters with notepads or recorders, roaming among the knots of excited citizens.

In spite of the loss of life suffered during the defense of the government, there was an air of celebration to the gathering in the plaza. Norberto Gorrell was loved by his people, and his courage in facing down the coup would only add to his legend. The victory over the last remnants of the Juarez cartel meant the cloud of the past had been lifted. The future was as full of possibilities as the cloudless sky.

Or was she thinking about her own future? In a way, it was still a blank page, but it was no longer daunting. She wouldn't be alone while she rebuilt her life.

Tyler belted one of the pair of terry-cloth robes that had come with the room and stepped onto the balcony. Eagle Squadron hadn't gone home as scheduled the night before. President Gorrell had personally invited them to enjoy the hospitality of the palace for an additional few days while he discussed the reclamation of the Juarez property with the major. Though the rest of the team had accepted, Tyler had preferred the privacy of the Royal Rocaman. Emily was pleased that he had. It seemed fitting to complete their time together in Rocama at the same place it had begun.

"Are you okay?" he asked.

She smiled. "What an odd question. I'd think I'd made that pretty obvious. I'm surprised the hotel management didn't send someone to investigate the noise, but if it would make you feel better, I'll scream a little louder the next time you do that particular thing with your fingers."

He chuckled, gave her a smacking kiss on her cheek and moved behind her to slip his arms around her waist. "You liked that, huh?"

"Gee, what was your first clue?"

"Maybe the scratches on my back?"

She turned her head. "Oh, no. I hadn't realized—"

"Relax. They were worth it." He kissed her nose, then leaned his cheek against her hair. "I was asking if you're okay about all the reporters down there."

She returned her gaze to the plaza while she considered her reply. The whole truth about the standoff with Kenyon had been withheld from the press. As before, Eagle Squadron's contribution to the resolution would never be known. And because of that, neither would the part Emily had played. On one level, it still bothered her. As a reporter, she disliked the idea of a cover-up, for any reason.

Yet most issues weren't black-and-white. There could also be value in words that were left unspoken.

"It's okay, Tyler," she said. "I might not be in on this story, but there will be other ones."

"I talked to the major. He has a few connections at the *Washington Post*."

"What? You're kidding."

"He doesn't kid. He'll put you in contact with them when we get back, if you want."

She hesitated. "As long as it doesn't mean I need to live in Washington."

"I thought as long as you had a computer and a phone, you could work pretty well anywhere."

"I suppose I could even work from Packenham Junction."

He tightened his grasp around her waist. "If you did,

I'd have a hell of a commute. Seeing as how my job isn't portable, it would make more sense if you moved in with me."

"We never really discussed that, did we?"

"What?"

"Moving in together is a big step. I told you I wasn't expecting a commitment or anything, so if you want to wait for a while—"

"Wait for what?" He turned her in his arms to face him. "I love you, Emily. My feelings aren't going to change, except to get stronger. I don't only want a girlfriend or a lover, I want a partner who'll be with me through the good times and the bad. Someone who's always on my side. Someone I trust with my heart."

"I want that, too."

"That's good, because I knew you were the woman for me from the moment we met."

"I was naked when we met."

He grinned. "Believe me, I noticed. So you can forget what you said about no commitments."

She laughed. "Are you giving me orders again, Sergeant?"

"No, only promises." He lifted her from her feet and backed through the balcony doors into their room. He released her when they got to the bed. His face sobered. "Emily, I'm not going to count our future in seconds or in minutes ever again." He stroked her hair from her cheeks and caught the back of her head. "Or in days or in weeks. I want a lifetime, because that's what I'm promising you."

Emily didn't want to move, or breathe. She wanted to cherish this moment when every dream she hadn't wanted to admit that she had was finally coming true.

She knew of no words that would do justice to the declaration Tyler had just made.

But given sixty or seventy years, she was bound to think of a few.

* * * * *

Want more EAGLE SQUADRON: COUNTDOWN?
Be sure to pick up ARMY OF TWO,
Major Redinger's story in August
from Ingrid Weaver and
Silhouette Romantic Suspense Books.

COMING NEXT MONTH

Available June 29, 2010

ROMANTIC SUSPENSE

REQUEST YOUR FREE BOOKS!

2 FREE NOVELS
PLUS
2 FREE GIFTS!

ROMANTIC
SUSPENSE

Sparked by Danger, Fueled by Passion.

YES! Please send me 2 FREE Silhouette® Romantic Suspense novels and my 2 FREE gifts (gifts are worth about $10). After receiving them, if I don't wish to receive any more books, I can return the shipping statement marked "cancel." If I don't cancel, I will receive 4 brand-new novels every month and be billed just $4.24 per book in the U.S. or $4.99 per book in Canada. That's a saving of 15% off the cover price! It's quite a bargain! Shipping and handling is just 50¢ per book.* I understand that accepting the 2 free books and gifts places me under no obligation to buy anything. I can always return a shipment and cancel at any time. Even if I never buy another book from Silhouette, the two free books and gifts are mine to keep forever.

240/340 SDN E5Q4

Name	(PLEASE PRINT)	
Address		Apt. #
City	State/Prov.	Zip/Postal Code

Signature (if under 18, a parent or guardian must sign)

Mail to the **Silhouette Reader Service:**

IN U.S.A.: P.O. Box 1867, Buffalo, NY 14240-1867
IN CANADA: P.O. Box 609, Fort Erie, Ontario L2A 5X3

Not valid for current subscribers to Silhouette Romantic Suspense books.

Want to try two free books from another line?
Call 1-800-873-8635 or visit www.morefreebooks.com.

* Terms and prices subject to change without notice. Prices do not include applicable taxes. N.Y. residents add applicable sales tax. Canadian residents will be charged applicable provincial taxes and GST. Offer not valid in Quebec. This offer is limited to one order per household. All orders subject to approval. Credit or debit balances in a customer's account(s) may be offset by any other outstanding balance owed by or to the customer. Please allow 4 to 6 weeks for delivery. Offer available while quantities last.

Your Privacy: Silhouette is committed to protecting your privacy. Our Privacy Policy is available online at www.eHarlequin.com or upon request from the Reader Service. From time to time we make our lists of customers available to reputable third parties who may have a product or service of interest to you. If you would prefer we not share your name and address, please check here. ☐

Help us get it right—We strive for accurate, respectful and relevant communications. To clarify or modify your communication preferences, visit us at www.ReaderService.com/consumerschoice.

SRS10R

HARLEQUIN®

A *Romance*

FOR EVERY MOOD™

Spotlight on
Heart & Home

Heartwarming romances
where love can happen
right when you least expect it.

See the next page to enjoy a sneak peek
from Silhouette Special Edition®,
a Heart and Home series.

CATHHSSE10

Introducing McFARLANE'S PERFECT BRIDE
by USA TODAY bestselling author Christine Rimmer,
from Silhouette Special Edition®.

Entranced. Captivated. Enchanted.

Connor sat across the table from Tori Jones and couldn't help thinking that those words exactly described what effect the small-town schoolteacher had on him. He might as well stop trying to tell himself he wasn't interested. He was powerfully drawn to her.

Clearly, he should have dated more when he was younger.

There had been a couple of other women since Jennifer had walked out on him. But he had never been entranced. Or captivated. Or enchanted.

Until now.

He wanted her—*her*, Tori Jones, in particular. Not just someone suitably attractive and well-bred, as Jennifer had been. Not just someone sophisticated, sexually exciting and discreet, which pretty much described the two women he'd dated after his marriage crashed and burned.

It came to him that he…he *liked* this woman. And that was new to him. He liked her quick wit, her wisdom and her big heart. He liked the passion in her voice when she talked about things she believed in.

He liked *her*. And suddenly it mattered all out of proportion that she might like him, too.

Was he losing it? He couldn't help but wonder. Was he cracking under the strain—of the soured economy, the McFarlane House setbacks, his divorce, the scary changes in his son? Of the changes he'd decided he needed to make in his life and himself?

SSEEXP0710

Strangely, right then, on his first date with Tori Jones, he didn't care if he just might be going over the edge. He was having a great time—having *fun*, of all things—and he didn't want it to end.

*Is Connor finally able to admit his feelings to Tori,
and are they reciprocated?
Find out in McFARLANE'S PERFECT BRIDE
by USA TODAY bestselling author Christine Rimmer.
Available July 2010,
only from Silhouette Special Edition®.*

Copyright © 2010 by Christine Reynolds

HARLEQUIN *Presents*

Bestselling Harlequin Presents® author

Penny Jordan

brings you an exciting new trilogy…

Needed:
THE WORLD'S MOST
ELIGIBLE
BILLIONAIRES

Three penniless sisters:
how far will they go to save the ones they love?

Lizzie, Charley and Ruby refuse to drown in their debts.
And three of the richest, most ruthless men in the world
are about to enter their lives. Pure, proud but penniless,
how far will these sisters go to save the ones they love?

Look out for

Lizzie's story—**THE WEALTHY GREEK'S**
CONTRACT WIFE, July

Charley's story—**THE ITALIAN DUKE'S**
VIRGIN MISTRESS, August

Ruby's story—**MARRIAGE: TO CLAIM HIS TWINS,**
September

www.eHarlequin.com

HP12927

Silhouette Desire

USA TODAY bestselling author

MAUREEN CHILD

brings you the first
of a six-book miniseries—
Dynasties: The Jarrods

Book one:

CLAIMING HER BILLION-DOLLAR BIRTHRIGHT

Erica Prentice has set out to claim
her billion-dollar inheritance
and the man she loves.

*Available in July
wherever you buy books.*

Always Powerful, Passionate and Provocative.

Visit Silhouette Books at www.eHarlequin.com

SD73037

HARLEQUIN®

INTRIGUE

**BESTSELLING
HARLEQUIN INTRIGUE AUTHOR**

DEBRA WEBB

**INTRODUCES THE LATEST
COLBY AGENCY SPIN-OFF**

COLBY AGENCY

MERGER

No one or nothing would stand in the way
of an Equalizer agent…but every Colby agent
is a force to be reckoned with.

Look for
COLBY CONTROL—*July*
COLBY VELOCITY—*August*

www.eHarlequin.com

HI69483